DE⌐

Jon Bladewake

Dead Prince

CONTENTS

Dead Prince

I. Spirits Made Flesh

As he wandered the steppes in search of safety, his skin scorched red and his garments mostly burned from him, he gazed up at the unsympathetic moon. In contemplation of that cold orb, he tried to purge from his mind the flames that had engulfed him only hours before. Soon after, he recollected the visage of the fiendish Hydran lord responsible for the attack, gloating over the ruin he had wreaked. He had only heard sketchy tales of the lords of Hydra. Though such an idea seemed unbelievable at first, Michael the wounded soldier now understood the truth of the incident. The murderous agent of evil responsible for the horrific crimes at the village was Lord Kraide Sephric. Kraide of the House of Sephric. The Sephrics were the ruling noble house of Hydra. They were said to share the same terrible ancestor, who was described as a demonic being alien to mankind.

Like many, Michael had come to consider the nefarious Sephrics as nothing more than a legend created to oblige the soldiers of Rose to fight harder. Such unforgivable evil was said to run in the veins of these men as would ensure they be received as spectres from the mind of a madman. Yet the unholy glow within that creature's eyes, like portals leading into the Undergrave's caverns of despair, had been unmistakable. The inhuman might of his musculature, the tallness of his frame, the sinister light in his visage, and the dark of his hair against his bloodlessly pale skin, affirmed that he was a member of the House of Sephric. He was a son of the legendary ruling family of Hydra. The words of Kraide, spoken to the mindless warrior slaves surrounding him, meant nothing to Rose ears: they sounded to Michael only as a grotesque babble with the unmistakable inflections of a curse. The language of Hydra was still a mystery, even to the best scribes and scholars of Rose. Never had there been dialogue between Rose and Hydra, nor had there ever been a lapse in the pure hatred and bloodshed between the two nations. Diplomacy was nonexistent between the two states.

Michael had certainly wanted to kill the Sephric lord, but he had found neither the courage nor the strength of body required to do so. He had slain warriors of Hydra many times before. And he and his companions had experienced no objections in their hearts when they killed them. Oddly, Michael had sometimes felt tender misgivings at the slaughter of animals, even if it had been necessary for his own nourishment. He had helped to farm rabbits as a young boy, and grew to like them. The inevitability of their slaughter had upset him. By such accounts, some would have thought him too compassionate, had they not heard of his fierce contributions to the security of the Rose Kingdom on the battlefield.

As Michael fled over windswept grass in the night, seeking as much distance as possible from the site of the atrocity, he remembered those recent agonising moments in the debris. Even in his state of terrible injury, he convinced himself that if only he had been able to move his body without such terrible pain, or if he had found the strength, he would have surely sprung out and tried to kill the Sephric oppressor with his bare scorched hands. Of course, he could never have assailed the mighty frame of his opponent successfully even if conditions had been more favourable. In spite of all their enemies, no-one had ever assassinated a Sephric before, even with far greater opportunities than Michael's. Rather than confronting his titanic foe, the scarred warrior had crawled away in hope of fighting another day. His body had been engulfed in flames, and he had miraculously fallen into the river, quenching the fire that had clung to his humble peasant garments. Only the man tending the watermill could have survived the events in the village that day, and that lone man was Michael.

He prayed that his body might prevail against the supernaturally inflicted burns, and wondered if something of his life might be salvageable. He could not still call himself *Michael of Loom*, for the village of Loom

7

was now nothing but strewn charcoal. That village was reduced, now, to a heap of ashes and the slain bodies of innocents. Those bodies, the escaped warrior believed, would be thrown to the various demonic war beasts the Hydrans brought with them and released upon the land. Only a bare few of the Hydran attackers had been killed by the villagers, struck down by the arrows dispatched from hunting bows. But the village had been taken by surprise, and massacre had been the only conceivable outcome. Such tragedies represent a frequent reality one must be prepared to face when resisting occupation by hostile forces in an era of barbarism and darkness.

As Michael thought about the nature of the attack, he discerned it was certainly not in accord with Hydran war doctrines for their raiding parties to venture this deep into the farmlands. The Hydrans had been wise not to make such bold strikes, because they had learned to fear harassment by the bands of fighters constantly pecking away at their supplies and reinforcements. But for a Sephric lord to come this far was unthinkable. Most would dismiss any such account as folly. If Michael survived, no-one would believe his story. It seemed impossible that a lord of the House of Sephric, one descended from that terrible ancient family, would risk himself by coming this far into hostile territory. If any Rose peasant learned of a Hydran lord's presence, any Rose villager bearing arms within two hundred leagues would have surely assembled like wolves. They would come for the head of a Sephric lord. No-one would refuse this opportunity to send a shaking message to the Hardrad, the King of Hydra, by killing his general Kraide.

In the course of the whole war, in all its carnage, no Sephric had ever fallen to the Rose. Though the brave fighters of Rose had slain thousands of Hardrad's soldiers, and even many of their mightiest war beasts, the Sephrics themselves had always proven unassailable. Although many Rose had sworn that they would kill such a monster to avenge their country's suffering, no Sephric had ever fallen. Michael had slain nearly a hundred Hydran soldiers, alongside his countrymen. Many called him a veteran of the war, even at the age of twenty-two, but he always assured his compatriots that his father's training and wisdom were the sole reasons for the exceptional skills he displayed.

After Michael had emerged from the river, he had understood how scarred his flesh was, and how terrible the red burns were. He believed he had been deformed for life. But as the pain intensified in his night wandering, he began to accept that he would surely succumb to these injuries. All of his hair had been burned from his head, leaving a scorched bald head. His eyelashes and eyebrows had been incinerated, and he had narrowly escaped blindness in the fire. How could he now walk to any friendly village, and expect to be greeted as a fellow native of Rose? How could his people recognise him as anything but a monstrous product of Hydran black magic and torture? All they would wish to do is to put him out of his misery, if they thought he still had a soul left at all.

Although he knew he would not have a happy fate, he did not weep for himself but for his dead sister Berenice. Michael's parents had died in the attack, but they were old. Their souls could accept what had happened. Although Michael had cared greatly for them, he knew that the death of his sister upset them far more than their own deaths. Why had her brother failed to protect her? When he closed his eyes, his mind delved into the memories of trivial childhood moments he had shared with his sister. And his pain at these memories was greater than anything inflicted by the fires of the hottest furnace. Her death was not a thing he ever thought he might face. He was a soldier. Surely it was his place to die first. Instead he had abandoned her, and escaped onto these steppes a shadow of the warrior he had been, doomed to die emasculated.

His skin and his soul were both in searing agony, and his eyes could not produce tears without stinging the adjacent burns torturously. So he wept quietly in pity for his sister, in such a way that would be as painful to any passerby as it was in his own heart. He was alone. And so he hoped to be alone forever. The world had forsaken him, and his own nation would forsake him if they could see him. The Hydrans would surely win, and all innocent things in the world would fall into darkness and mockery. Compassion would die finally, at the hands of these monsters. With all hope gone, he grieved for the final defeat of Rose. He took his sister's suffering as the omen of such misfortune.

The pain in his skin and flesh persisted, and it seemed to grow more intense. Dark grey clouds were overhead and the air was warm. A violent storm approached from the north. The storms always carried the most fierce thunder and lightning from Hydra, beyond the Forbidden Mountains. It had been said that the magicians of Hydra were capable of invoking the power of demons that could master the weather, bringing these disastrous storms against Rose. Many dismissed such an idea as a fairytale, or a legend that had been sown to add to the dread everyone already felt at the mere mention of the name of Hydra. Michael had known those storms from the north all his life, just as he had known the merciless enemy from the north. They did not frighten him, but he knew that they could be deadly if he did not find shelter, so he crept into the shadow of a cave's mouth in the roots of the mountains, and there he remained.

Dead Prince

He was sure the horror of the attack on the village would plague him forever, as if a thousand fire spirits had taken up residence in his flesh to torment his soul, and they would cling to his soul, even after death. The flames, the heat and the choking fumes, so close and encircling, had reduced him to a helpless animal in the ruins of the village. Five years of combat experience against the Hydrans had not desensitised him enough to keep his fortitude that day. Searching his mind, he postulated a final and ultimate philosophy of war; an answer that waits for the soldier at the end of history. This philosophy teaches that there is a soldier who cannot be defeated. But he must be the one who shows fortitude through any pain, and is devoted to kill the enemy, no matter his own sufferings or the likelihood of his impending death. The soldier is an instrument only, and has no thought of survival or return. He has a central and exclusive objective. Nothing can prevent his sword from dealing its destined strike, and it needs to strike only once. This soldier is bound to an errand of doom, and has already committed to the rationale that a single, evidently attainable deed is the only reason he was born. Such an assassin would be aware, throughout his every action, that the destruction of Rose at the hands of the evil King Hardrad is a more terrible outcome than the most severe pain that could be inflicted upon any one man. So his life would mean nothing in this struggle against evil. Burning to death, Michael had been told, is the most painful sensation. He had witnessed that. He had witnessed that to an extent few survive to tell of. And if he could transcend the experience and emerge a soldier once more, he might even find abilities great enough to finally rise up and slay the lords of Hydra.

In the hollow where he slept after his excruciating limp to shelter that day, Michael dreamt a strange and disturbing dream. In the depths of the dream, he saw his burned raw flesh again, and felt the same pain that he had known when he was awake, just hours before. He looked at the burns, and worried again about their permanence and the threat of torment until death. But, as if by some trick of sorcery, the burns vanished, and the health of his skin and flesh was not only restored, but went even stronger. But despite this healing, the same agony continued to devour and corrupt his flesh like fire, as it had done before. Unable to ignore the horrific and unbearable discomfort of his delicate skin and flesh, Michael woke with a cry of pain several times during the night. But, each time, he subsequently fell back into his slumber. In each chapter of the dream he managed to gather, he experienced a fragment of the whole message. People forget the details of dreams. But, if one can wake at a point before the dream reaches its conclusion, its inconclusiveness prompts us to contemplate it deeper in ouf conscious minds and so retain memory of its details. Michael remembered his dream's message in great detail, because the dream was incomplete upon each of his successive awakenings. After he witnessed each chapter of the whole dream, he could think about it and interpret its symbolism, until he was certain he had deciphered a strange message contained within.

Ignoring the repeated visions of his own healing flesh, from which he ascertained no particular message, Michael came to understand a certain revelation within the dream. This very cave was not simply a hole in the roots of the mountains. There was a certain shadowy fissure in the rock at the cave interior's limit to the east. Beyond that channel, he would find a deeper cavern, which would conceal him in complete darkness. Michael was instantly suspicious of the possibility some fearsome creature lurking there, brought from Hydra to infest the lands of Rose. The thought of that deeper hollow scared him deeply, and made him believe the primary cave must be dangerous too, although it was certainly not as dangerous as the Hydran storm raging outside. When he finally woke, the fighter understood the last image he received in his dream. There was an extensive labyrinth of burial vaults beyond the cave, and they could be directly accessed through a crypt beyond the secondary hollow. It would require Michael's passage through the fissure and that dark secondary cavern, until he saw a warm orange light inviting him onward. There were candles, still burning in the crypt. Candles in memory of men centuries-dead? Perhaps by means of some mischievous technique of sorcery, they still burned.

The only wizards capable of sustaining fire for centuries and perpetuating things that should have perished long ago were those agents of a mysterious order known as Transpathic Monks. They were a greatly feared cult, whose origins were said to date back thousands of years. Though Michael had little knowledge of them, he knew enough to make him afraid. It was said that they held similar supernatural abilities to the magicians of Hydra, and that they understood the same infernal powers. The sinister Order of Transpathy was immersed in a Dark Realm of science, which had made its agents devoid of compassion. Although they were of the Rose Kingdom, the Transpathic Monks had never used their powers to help their benevolent state in times of war as Hydran magicians had done for their nation. But much of the knowledge about Hydra's black sorcery and forbidden science, as the Rose had come to understand, had come from the extensive manuscripts of the Transpathic Monks, whose scholars were oft described as the greatest in the world.

A strange revelation had been transmitted to Michael in the stream of enigmatic images and sensations arriving by way of his dream. If he did not seek out the Transpathic Monks, he believed, he would soon die. Surely only they possessed enough knowledge of forbidden arts to heal his horrible injuries before he finally succumbed to the demonic fire brought into his flesh by Hardrad's legion of magicians. All depended upon him reaching these holy men before he succumbed. But this perilous course would mean travelling through the black hollow waiting beyond the fissure.

Michael knew that any number of monstrous creatures could be lurking in the secondary cavern beyond the fissure, hungering for a passing victim. But his fears of concealed Hydran serpents were overwhelmed by his desire to pass, for those fears were not enough to overwhelm his eagerness to remedy the pain his skin's sears were forcing upon him. He limped across the cave's dark stone, barely able to see through the enveloping black. Only the faintest trace of moonlight was finding its way into the cave from the entrance, and reflecting on pools and stones to provide the ever-so-faint illumination necessary for his sight and his passage. An occasional strike of lightning would send light intruding deep, and help him see deeper into the hollow. And one such strike of illumination revealed to him the reality behind his dream, for it revealed the dark fissure. It was, of course, the same fissure from the dream, in evidence before him. It bade his passage through its narrow doorway. It would take him into the damp interior of the secondary hollow, where he would travel through a cavernous black realm of dreaded concealment.

The perilous fissure in the rock was not an appealing entrance, and Michael hesitated, knowing that it would take him into the concealment of a vast and unsafe cavern. He grabbed the rock for stability, as he stepped forward through the fissure, and felt its coarseness inflict severe torment upon his blistering palms. Enduring his body's suffering, he stepped forward into the darkness of the hollow. He could not see inside it. Its reality terrified him, for he now knew the reality the rest of the dream, including the labyrinth of stone tunnels and vaults waiting for his passage. He moved with great caution, on his blistering hands and feet, so that he would not walk into some natural obstruction of rock in the hollow. The darkness kept him ignorant of the true size of the hollow, and he did not wish to linger, because he had nothing but dread and uncertainty with regard to its possible concealed occupants. He clawed his way, even though his hands and knees were so terribly sore, and he was uncertain if he should hasten or go cautiously, for he wished to limit his time in the hollow to a bare minimum, but he also dreaded that he might fall into some chasm and perish there, if he should hasten.

To his relief, the wounded warrior soon reached beyond the hollow, and believed that there may perhaps have been no threat there after all. But he was by no means certain of the safety of the vast hollow he left behind. In fact, there was one thing that had cultivated a chilling sensation in Michael's spine as he moved through that cavern. He remembered that he experienced the faintest sound of irritated breathing, and he attributed it neither to man nor one of nature's creatures. But, after it had subsided, the haunted soldier could not be certain if it was even the sound of breathing, at all. Perhaps it may have been some faint whisper of the wind, channelled through another fissure connected to the outside. Michael had no interest in finding out, for he had wanted only to reach the other side of the hollow. The whole experience in the hollow did seem eerie, and he blamed neither the raging storm nor his own accursed mental and physical injuries. Whatever might have been concealed in that darkness, he knew that his only chance of survival was waiting in the labyrinth beyond it. He had reached the entrance to the crypt in his dream, for he could see the yellow glow of his invitation. It radiated from the candles lit and magically perpetuated by the monks.

The coldness and the scars of the ruined shell he called his body made him eager to reach the candles, whose light made the crypt look very warm and inviting. He limped across the last expanse of rock in the dark, and exited the hollow, and subsequently rested. He contemplated his strait under the candlelight of the crypt. There was a stone passage that led away from the crypt, inviting him away into the labyrinth. Candles lit all the way, and they never diminished. The wounded warrior rushed passed one of them and it flickered, but it did not go out. Although he was curious to know the results, he would not mockingly test the place by attempting to put out one of the candles. He was certain supernatural activity was taking place here, and he knew it is unwise to be in proximity to, let alone to disturb, a supernatural process you do not understand. The candles were of many different sizes, yet they showed no sign of diminishing, as if they were enchanted to burn eternal. Michael was sure, because of the painfully realised truth of the relationship between magic and fire, that a spell had been placed here many years ago. It may even have been a century since any human had walked in the shadowy place. The candles might have been burning in memory of the first Rose lives that were lost in the battle with the armies of Hydra.

Only when he saw some ancient skeletal remains resting on the stone floor of the passage, did Michael begin to suspect that something sinister might dwell in this place, and be readying an unhappy fate for him. Michael was desperately hoping that he would encounter the Transpathic Monks, if anything so they might put him out of his misery or bring about the completion of his dark destiny. If fate chose to let him live, the sinister monks would find him and heal him, by their mysterious powers, if they had any sense of pity. However, he wandered through the catacombs for many hours, without encountering anyone, and saw the sarcophagi of Rose soldiers who died in great battles long ago. They were possibly some of the first warriors fallen to the armies of Hydra.

Michael had heard stories of encounters between the living and the sleepless spirits of the dishonoured dead. He rushed on, not desiring an encounter of this kind, for he had nothing to say to the dead, and did not want to hear a word from them now, for he believed that he was soon to dwell among them. He had the most peculiar feeling of dread and remorse until he became aware of the reason why destiny had guided him here, and it brought tears to his eyes, which tortured his suffering skin once more. The dead, here, were his ancestors, and they were displeased with him. They thought him cowardly and dishonourable. His desperation to escape death in the path of the Hydran foe had made him abandon the opportunity to assassinate a Sephric, as any other Rose in his predicament would have been brave enough to attempt. The dead were immensely disappointed that he had not taken his chance to slay Lord Kraide. It had been his duty to move into blind rage and kill the foe.

'My judgment was impaired by my injuries!' Michael said aloud, in a tremulous voice, conscious that a nearby spirit could hear him and was judging him.

'You have dishonoured yourself and your sister!' a horrible voice said, and Michael recoiled in terror. It was his father, who had died only hours earlier, many miles away from here.

'No! I couldn't! My injuries depleted my strength! I possessed no remaining vitality to fight!'

'You should have tried, or you should have stayed and perished there as a soldier should. You disappoint me. You have failed to defend your sister. Your flight and your abandonment of her have destroyed you. I will never forgive you for this.'

'To kill a Sephric Lord is not possible. They are immortal.'

'No. It is possible for those who have courage. You were the first of us who had a real chance. You were an able marksman of the bow. And there were many weapons strewn about. You should have taken that chance, and given your life for Rose. Look at what you have become now. You will never die in battle with your sword in your hand. You're a coward. Only pain and death waits for you.'

'Father, you must forgive me. If you understood the truth of that situation, you would not inflict this vindictive curse on me,' Michael choked, but the ghost would speak no more, because it had forsaken him. He continued through the corridor of stone, carrying shame and immense regret that he had not perished with his sister. He would never have the chance to redeem himself, even in death. As he walked onward through the stone corridor in the yellow candlelight, his head hanged in bitter remorse and all his strength invested into resisting his tears, his passage was suddenly blocked by a dark robed figure. He jumped back in fright, and saw only the line of a sour mouth when he tried to look at the stranger's face.

'You will regret this intrusion, wretched creature. This place is known only to the Order of the Transpaths.'

'Please,' Michael said, approaching the stranger. In an instant, the monk revealed a sharp blade from his robes, and it was immediately pressed at one of Michael's jugular veins. One swish of the blade would entail his bleeding to death at the first sign of trouble, so he remained motionless and silent. The monk would control this conversation.

'Explain what became of you,' the monk croaked, his face coming very close to Michael's as if to inspect his scorched visage in great detail, and Michael saw the narrow and piercing eyes which were black and unreadable, and contained the strangest glint of otherworldly wisdom in them.

'I'm a villager. My name is Michael,' he answered in a cautious quiet voice. The warrior now sounded as harmless and yielding as a sacrificial lamb.

After the name was said, the monk's blade immediately vanished back into his robe and the threat of execution was gone. 'You are alone?' the monk asked.

'I am. My village has been destroyed, and–'

'I can see this,' the monk said in a strong and penetrating voice, with such religious authority that Michael developed an intense fear of his judgment. 'You are in need of aid, and I can give it to you, if you pass our test. I am Guidonis.'

'What kind of test? You must explain this. I do not understand.'

'Of course you don't, you fool! Now you must keep your mouth shut and follow me. I must get you into the church at once, if I am to treat your injury. Don't look any other agent of the Order in the eye. Keep your eyes on me, and I will bring you safely to the church in the depths of the mountain. We must move quickly. I can only help you when we reach it.'

II. Origins of the Curse

Nothing could have warned the Kingdom of the Rose of their inevitable vendetta with the warlike neighbouring realm. To their north, beyond the great boundary of haunting forests called the Grave Expanse and the cold heights of the Forbidden Mountains, there was a frozen and accursed wilderness inhabited by ferocious beasts that would tear a man to shreds as soon as he set foot upon it. And yet the Hydrans had emerged from beyond these feared frontiers of the north. No man of the Rose ever dared to venture that far north. Not even the most courageous scout set himself on that dark road to trace the origin of the aggressor's legions, for it was forbidden. It was said with a quivering tongue, even by those who were the wisest and most learned in the great mysteries of the world, that no man of the Rose who chooses that perilous course shall return.

The sigil of the barbarians of the north was an abominable black serpent, possessed of many hissing heads. This detail led them to be known to the Rose by the dreaded name of the *Kingdom of the Hydra*. Their fierce "people" were a legion of warrior slaves called the *Hydrans*, and their lives were dedicated to an endless war on the rest of the world. No other realm whose mention has survived in our history books can be compared with that aggressive state. Perhaps they can only be called villainy, because there is no better word. They seemed to be a host of mercenaries, sorcerers, and madmen, as though all the people who belong in the worst depths of torment in the Undergrave flocked to their banner and made an army of hideous damned souls. They were driven by an uncompromising desire to see all other nations perish by their swords, and this single occupation was the exclusive focus of praise in their heinous culture.

All of the Hydrans were sworn to partake in endless warfare against humanity, concerned with neither honour nor restraint. Their altered bodies were aided by curses in battle, and evil filled their eyes. The structure of their society beyond the frontier was a mystery. No mother or child of Hydra was known to exist. Evidence showed the Rose that their foes were only male warriors, capable of immense inhuman strength. Battle magic bound them together, so that even in death they were still capable of rising and fighting until their whole bodies were utterly destroyed by their foes. They were slaves to a cult of war. It was the highest injunction of their nameless maker to bring misery and destruction upon all outside realms.

When the war was new, the Kingdom of the Rose possessed no armies to defend against Hydra's relentless hordes. And, in the course of the original Hydran incursion, they were subjected to cruelties like nothing they might have witnessed in their nightmares prior. They had always been a society of simple shepherds and farmers, who lived in defenceless villages with their companions and their children. They loved their neighbours, they heard nothing of wars or grief, and they craved no power.

The dark days began during a particularly terrible year, which chronicled many mysterious plagues and disasters, when raiding parties speaking a strange untranslatable tongue came to the lands of the Rose. The invading barbarians seemed less interested in stealing their lands and property than in simply murdering them and taking possession of their bodies. They left everyone in their path dead and eerily ravaged, some with unknown glyphs carved into their flesh, still others partially cannibalised. A wave of rumours of unspeakable violations, including talk of the sleepless dead, swept through the lands of the Rose. Worse than the terror birthed by the slaughter and sacrificial ritual mutilation, the Hydrans left the scourges of disease, witchcraft and black magic everywhere they went. Cremation of all the dead, friend or foe, became the norm among the Rose. For they feared the necromancy practiced by the warrior magicians of Hydra, by which there had already arisen sleepless legions of the exhumed in the darkest days of the war.

The Rose, who had never known hate, were forced to learn it very quickly. The cursed warriors of the demoniac horde of Hydra were not creatures one could show compassion towards. So long as their bodies remained mobile, they used all their existence to spread death and ruin to others. In the dark pits of their eyes there was an insatiable malice no life-driven being is capable of, for their bodies were no more than the ravaged mounts of evil spirits.

The Kingdom of the Rose was facing a reckless army of inexorable destroyers unlike anything that had marched before. The formerly peaceful deity worshipped in the Kingdom of the Rose, a being they called their Constructor, soon became their guarantor of vengeance and sanctioned the spilling of all Hydran blood. The religious hymns and tales of the Rose were transformed to respond to their terrible plight, and their whole culture birthed an undying aspiration to destroy the invader. Though it took many years enduring unspeakable atrocities beyond count, the people of the Rose were fortunate that bands of courageous villagers began to fight back. The small community of hunters fared better than their shepherd and farmer brethren, because they hunted the Hydrans by bow, much as they had hunted various creatures in their land for meat. But, despite their increasing losses, the Hydrans were not discouraged. They were a legion using every moment of its existence to pursue destruction and suffering, so they felt ever more drawn to the Rose because that state resisted them. And what was once a series of minor raids quickly escalated into a full-scale invasion.

The small bands of Rose could not resist such an invasion through direct and open battle, because the Hydrans possessed superior armour and a hideous cavalry force mounted on exotic serpentine monsters to ride down their victims in the open field. Determined to outwit their foes, the Rose instead formed a highly disciplined guerrilla army over the years, trained to ambush Hydran supply wagons and the monstrous mounts of their cavalrymen in difficult terrain, crippling their superior foes. The heavy Hydran forces were diffused into the rural expanse, where they proved incapable of the rapid and concentrated devastation their war doctrines commanded them to inflict.

But even when they saw that they were faced with tough bands of foes and unsuitable lands for their doctrine of war, the Hydrans cared not for their casualties, and continued to pour their soldiers to their dooms, because their rulers appeared to hold them as nothing more than worthless slaves. The Hydran rulers also clearly believed that the subjugation of Rose would be a triumph so great that it would outweigh any conceivable losses. Rose stood in the way of the southern road, and such a realm blocked the potential passage of the armies of Hydra in their descent upon the rest of the world. The valiant Kingdom of the Rose stood directly south of Hydra's icy wastes, and there existed no potential road around these lands by which the aggressor could expand. And so, fuelled by Hydra's limitless tenacity, the war dragged on for a century, and the Hydrans brought their most sinister weapons to bear against the Rose. Pernicious plagues and atrocious black magic. They unlocked forbidden forms of sorcery to invoke many a species of evil spirit to lay waste to the lands of Rose. Among them, they brought pretas, maggots, basilisks and fire knights, and such death-beings would do mischief and torment to any Rose village they found. The prayers of the Rose were unanswered. Again and again, they were smitten by a legion of spirits made flesh, which should rightfully have been confined to the darkness of the Undergrave and never permitted to wander the Earth.

One atrocity involved unholy beings of an uncertain nature, known as the pretas. They were summoned by Hydran magicians and proceeded to cultivate torment by fire in the village of Loom. It was during this incident that the family of a resistance fighter named Michael perished in terrible agony by the unnatural flames, and the man himself experienced the torments of the same heat as he watched them perish. The burning of the skin is the most terrible pain that can scourge human flesh. Michael now possessed the knowledge of such fire, for it had mortally scourged his body and soul just as it had slain his mother, his father and his sister. The burns had corrupted him, and their corruption had pervaded his whole body, so that he possessed only hours before death.

...

Because the warnings of Guidonis in the ancient labyrinth terrified him, Michael obeyed the commands of the monk. As he followed the mysterious stranger fearfully, his eyes were fixed on the black robes flowing behind him, and he did not dare once to lift his head to look at the surrounding hall of stone, despite his powerful curiosity to do so, for he knew that it would be against the warnings of Guidonis. He knew this place was deep beneath the rock of the earth, and that their way was lit only by torch and candlelight. Somehow, he could feel the other monks watching him. His ominous feelings were telling him the inhabitants of this temple at the mountain's heart weren't quite human, and that a terrible fate would await him if he was bold enough to discard the bizarre warnings of Guidonis by laying eyes upon them.

Michael remembered short verses from the oldest chronicles of Rose, and he knew enough to discern that the Transpathic monks had their shadowy origins in the earliest chapters of the history of his realm. Even old-wives-tales had oft referred to the Order of Transpathy, when they sought to explain the tragic and mysterious disappearances of young children who wandered too far from home. And, indeed, Michael now suspected that there might be significant truths within such hearsay. Were these vanished children, perhaps, taken by magicians to remote mountain hideouts, and educated there in dark otherworldly arts? Were they turned into those magicians' apprentices, some of whom even lived centuries-long lives, sustained by unspeakable ways of heretical sorcery? Yet the Rose had never descended in a pogrom against the Order. Legend told of Transpathic intervention against far more sinister forces. Perhaps the Order existed to intervene against darker forces that posed a far greater threat to innocents. What they did, then, was the alternative to a far more terrible evil; the Rose needed a peculiar element extracted from their people, to be specially conditioned into inhumanity. Some might argue that an inhuman enemy demands that one strips some of his own soldiers of their humanity, so they might confront the greater evil. The rumours regarding the Order of Transpathy preceded the invasions by the northern barbarians of Hydra. The historic interventions of dark forces against the Rose preceded the Hydran invasions, and so perhaps also did the Transpathic Order's solutions to these scourges precede the coming of Hardrad's armies.

As Michael travelled in the labyrinth of rock, the sufferings of his skin were almost eased by the stillness of his quiet and dry surroundings. It was warm, but not too warm. He regretted that he could not observe this underground architectural wonder properly, because he could only have his eyes on the flowing robe of the monk, in accord with his promise not to make eye contact with any of the inquisitive brothers of Guidonis.

Passing through an iron door, which was adorned with the traditional winged cross, his national symbol, the monk led Michael into a large chamber. The door slammed shut behind them, and Michael knew that it had not been closed by hand. It had either been drawn shut by the otherworldly forces present, or it had responded to the mind of Guidonis, whose powers permeated the whole place.

'You are free to look now,' Guidonis told Michael, and he spun apprehensively in observation the imposing stone surroundings. He found that he had been led inside a curious subterranean place, which contained an altar and was of a templar kind of architecture. He could have mistaken its interior for that of a normal church, but it lacked the decor of stained glass windows, for what use would they be in the darkness underneath the earth? With no such windows providing illuminating beams for the worshipper, there were instead flickering torches.

The monk instructed Michael to kneel, and he obeyed. As he did so, he hesitated to look at Guidonis again, because he was fearful and uncertain. But, finally, he did begin to turn his bloodshot eyes up and regard the shadowy face of the monk. The conjurer's dark eyes were still unblinking and stern as they examined him, betraying his possession of great wisdom. He shouted something in another tongue, and it was not Hydra's foul language, but something else. Even though the monk was not an agent of the enemy, those words scared Michael, because they resembled the incantations of Hydra's fearsome magicians. The soldiers of Rose had learned, long ago, to fear the oral curses from Hydra's arsenal of sorcery, because they were not ignorant of the fact that so many nations and armies had surely fallen to them.

'I demand to know what you are doing to me,' Michael said, upon realising that Guidonis might be trying to use him as some kind of sacrificial victim in a horrific ritual. But his words had not left his mouth. He only believed that he had attempted to utter them. Somehow, he had been silenced by the monk's incantations. In terror, he tried to jump to his feet and flee, but his body betrayed him. He remained kneeled. His limbs refused to serve him, and they remained in place as if they now only obeyed the monk's commands.

'I will answer your question,' Guidonis said, 'you are undergoing a transformation. It is the only possible treatment that will allow you to continue living.'

'Sorcery?' Michael mouthed in horror, certain that he did not want to be subjected to more of the unnatural and obscene sciences of death and destruction by otherworldly means. These sciences had already destroyed his precious family, and he wanted nothing more to do with them. Man should not meddle with forces he does not understand, in his reckless desire to smite his enemies. It might make him powerful, but should also serve to inevitably turn him into a monster.

'You are already dead, mortal. And so you will become powerful. One cannot kill what does not live!' the monk replied.

'What is this madness supposed to accomplish?' Michael tried to express.

'A disease has come into your flesh. You are dying from the outside in. The burns are killing you. And not only this. An ongoing form of Hydran sorcery is still affecting your flesh, young mortal. Pretas are inside your flesh, consuming you from the inside out. *Outside in, inside out!* Death is fast approaching you! I will do nothing but take this lump of mortal flesh you call a body, for I say that I can turn it into something useful again. Perhaps it can become a sword to slay the enemy we share.'

'I will not become an instrument of further heresy!'

The conjurer ceased to discuss the situation with Michael. Instead, he uttered many more strange words, and their intonation was foreboding. The fires diminished. An evil presence was surely being drawn into the chamber.

The same vicious screeching sounds, which had tormented Michael incessantly during the attack on his village, returned to scourge his ears. *Pretas*. The monk was right. So the conjurer was drawing them out of his flesh. Fiery wings, which came like the flare of hellish bats, flashed around the room in a perilous torrent from his body, paralysing him with dread. There came a storm of shadow and flame. There were demoniac cries from an everlasting inferno. Michael's skin burned as he endured the exorcist's surgery. And surgery means pain, he reminded himself. Michael revisited a strange childhood memory, in which his father dug a splinter from the tip of his finger. It had been trivial in comparison with wounds he had sustained in combat, but as a child he had found it extremely agonising. He concentrated on the logic of the matter. Perhaps the ways of Guidonis meant a similar solution, but it was for a far worse injury. However painful he may have found it as a child, the removal of that splinter had been mundane. This injury was unnatural, and its treatment was equally so. Yet, still, with his teeth gritted, he withstood the severe agony of this unbelievable act of surgical exorcism, until all of his flame-winged tormentors were gone. They were cast into a void that Michael could not see. They vanished into the church's walls, as if they were shut away and imprisoned in the stone.

With the disappearance of these fiery entities, the warm glow of the lamps returned to the room. And, although he was still bound by Guidonis's sorcery, so that he was unable to escape from his kneeling position, Michael was certain that the exorcist treatment was working. He decided that he should no longer resist nor impede the work of the heretic monk. He would not question his healer again, until his work was done.

'*Michael,*' the high haunting call of some spectral woman sounded from behind him. Michael did not recognise it at once. It was surely impossible that a woman could be found in the forbidden places of the Transpaths, unless she was needed for some specific ritual purpose that demanded a female victim.

A dazzling light penetrated the room from all its corners, and some form of enchanted fire was sent forth from the cracks. It broke the mortar asunder and sent an arc of lightning into Michael, flattening him against the floor as powerfully as a charging horse. Disoriented, he stood up again in the room, which seemed much larger. It was distorted in form. It was apparently rocking from side to side, as if it had become a compartment in a ship sailing stormy seas, or inside an unstable structure on the verge of collapse. Guidonis was no longer present, although Michael believed this was not possible, for the monk had seemed so determined to complete the ritual. This vision could only mean his own soul was being projected elsewhere whilst his body remained on the church floor. It seemed as though he was unconscious, yet retained his awareness of the church's interior. Michael dismissed what he saw. It was surely a dream or a hallucination, because his head felt so light that his imagination might conjure up anything and have him believe it to be as real as the foundations of the earth.

The locked iron door was thrown open, and figures entered by it, to join him in the church's interior. Hearing this, he turned around in terror, and thought his doom was at hand, but he recognised the three faces of his household. At first, his reunion with them brought indescribable joy to his heart. They were the spectres of his mother, his father, and his sister. But their faces were in unrest and sorrow, because of the pain in their hearts, and their bodies bore the terrible injuries of their slaughter in the village. How had it come to pass, that such innocent people could be slaughtered? How could it be that such harmless beings are stamped out like insects, their lives of bliss ended in an orgy of hatred and malice? Their ultimate fate had been realised as their reduction to nothing more than carcasses for scavengers, morsels for beasts of war to chew on like dogs at the discarded bones from some roast. Their bodies had become fuel for a war of total extermination on their fellows. They had proven to be not even a minor obstacle to the enemy, but a resource to accelerate Hardrad's conquest of the lands of Rose. Surely there was no defence against the agents of such overwhelming, all-devouring malice. As Michael looked into these familiar eyes, tears stung his own. He regarded their mortal injuries in terror, the killing blows dealt by the merciless soldiers of General Kraide.

Michael's spirit sank into the smothering cold and dark as he saw the contusions on Berenice's neck, which indicated that she had been suffered an excessively violent death by some horrifying means of suffocation. She was his sister. In his most tranquil memories, she was always a small girl who stood out with her green eyes, her rosy cheeks and her long red hair. Even after she had grown up and was no longer a child, Michael still saw her as an object of his defence. It was, in a way, to preserve her that he fought so hard. The girl's soul had expressed the real manner of her beauty, because she was so selflessly kind in life. And yet, despite all the goodness and peace that she had epitomised for her brother, it had been rewarded only with suffocation at the hands of a pack of vicious Hydran soldiers.

In spite of all the traumatic cruelties Berenice's body had been subjected to, her raw celestial being was presently judging him with a look of grace, strength and wisdom, as though she had been granted sainthood and so attained power in death. It was not Michael who reached out to comfort the spirit of a woman following her untimely death. It was she, in her martyrdom, who was the imposing one, with a look of pity for him. Her pity for him was far more than he could possibly return. Michael did not look directly into her eyes, for he knew that his knees would forcibly bend him and he would find himself kneeling. He had never quite felt such reverence for her while she lived, but now, as a martyr in communication with him, she was truly blessed with powers of light that could not be questioned by any human soul. It would be blasphemous for him, the wretched and scarred survivor, condemned by his father, to presume to speak first.

His mother had been taken by several arrows at her waist. But Michael's father had the worst injury, for it was of a kind that had certainly targeted his soul itself for fiery torments, as well as his body. A great cavity had been burned away inside his chest, by the ravenous pretas, like a collection of maggots discovered within an apple. Michael knew that their bodies no longer bore these physical injuries, for, certainly, once dead, more horrific damage and complete destruction had followed. However, the appearances before him were as the souls had known their bodies at the point when they departed.

Now, as he looked on their injuries, they studied his. 'You have perished in dishonour. You have been irreversibly condemned, because of your abandonment of your sister in the village,' his father said, in a voice that only expressed unparalleled doom and surrender.

Michael could not tolerate his father's stubborn condemnation of him, which he knew was the result of the manner of the untimely death, for it had turned him into a restless spirit, so the son had to break his silence and address the father. 'But I do have a chance to redeem myself, if the monk should heal me!' But, as he said those words, Michael was struck by what seemed to be a dreamlike vision of his scarred and bald-headed corpse lying on the church floor, lifeless and infested with evil. Was he already just another victim of the extraordinary powers mobilised by Hydra, just like his fallen sister?

Not so, for the heretical monk's ritual was still underway. The monk was aware of the presence of Michael's projecting spirit, although the latter felt like a pair of eyeballs floating, in a drunken state, about the concealed stone of the church's interior. There was a cyclic sound of demoniac shrieks and howls, now, quiet, behind the stone walls that enclosed the church. These were the cries of the evil preta spirits, still unrestrained in their death-mongering hunger and all-consuming heat. They were agents of torment in death, whose deserved place was the Undergrave. But they were safely encased away, in stone, for now, where they could plague him no longer.

With the pretas imprisoned in stone, and his body lying there, a helpless ingredient in this unholy alchemy, the heretic began the most fascinating and previously unimaginable part of the ritual. He was touching every surface of Michael's body, such that Michael felt, for one moment, that he was the victim of some rite developed by minds of scandalous perversion. This did make Michael wonder if it was all merely a scam, excused by promises that had been founded in pseudoscience and held no powers against the real art of sorcery that was still tormenting his flesh. If it was so, he would die, and he was not to be the instrument the monk claimed to be anointing for a special purpose.

Although the outcome was far better than the fate that he had feared, he was disturbed to discover that the ritual was not based upon nonsense and pseudoscience, and was truly magical. In fact, the chanting and the groping was integral to the ritual, for it was doing something incredible to Michael's seemingly lifeless body. His skin appeared to be being *cleansed* of its scars, as if they were no more than a layer of impurities on the exterior of his body. As the evidence of melting, scarring and severe blistering was wiped from his flesh, his body acquired a new complexion that it had never possessed, even at the height of its health. The burns were not replaced by the skin of a newborn baby, as he half suspected, in his momentary prejudices about the outcome of this occult healing. Instead, his flesh looked dark, as if from much time spent under the sun, and well-toned as if from significant exercise. It was surely older skin than he had lost in his injuries in the village. And, as his scalp regenerated, no hair replaced what had been lost in the village's destruction. It was such that a quite healthy, although hairless, head developed, but it bore the same face that Michael had once possessed, despite the change of complexion. It was surely made from the flesh of another, but it was a body made for him to inhabit. It was his body, only with the skin of another. Only now, as he realised that his body had wondrously healed, did he dare to look at his sinister healer again.

His healer, he was quite confused and horrified to discover, was violently quaking with agony, before he collapsed onto his knees, and subsequently fell forward, now a severely burned and melted man beneath his robes, just as Michael had been, prior to the ritual. As he witnessed his healer's last moments, Michael tried to understand what had happened, and only concluded that something had gone horribly wrong and had *backfired* on the sorcerer. Whatever had gone wrong, he thought, would result in a disaster that would surely leave both of their souls in a very tortured state forever. Why had he put his faith in black sorcery and those who presume to boldly wield it in the name of good? It had been doomed! Black sorcery is loyal to its *Master*. The Devil's instruments serve the Devil's ends.

However, he subsequently discovered that it had not been so. For, as he drifted, like a pair of slimy astral eyeballs, perhaps swimming in some place where the viscous River Styx intersects the spheres of temporality, but can only permit sight and not touch, he slipped violently back into his own skull and opened his eyes in horrified uncertainty. In that moment of re-imprisonment into his brain, he saw that some other beings had been liberated at the precise moment when he was shut away into his body. The pretas darted from the wall like fiery arrows, shrieking as if they were some needy supernatural pets in want of their master, and funnelled down the burnt corpse of the heretic, by his mouth, which went alight and quickly filled the room with smoke, as Michael stamped frantically on the robes to put out the flames. When he had suffocated the pretas by denying them access to the air that they require to burn, he was further perplexed to find that no corpse remained in the robes of the deceased monk. Only ashes remained. In his confusion, his mind was presently unable to develop sympathy for the monk who had been immolated in the course of saving his life. It had *backfired*. The monk was probably trying to kill him. He was determined only to escape from this perilous place. Hardly able to believe the convenience of the strange outcome, he could see no more fitting choice of garments than those robes, if he hoped to slip away, unhindered by the guardian monks, who had proven to be paranoid of outsiders, especially those who may be contaminated by alien forms of sorcery.

Those black robes were strangely unaffected by the burning of their owner's body within them. No doubt, this was due to the function of pretas in devouring a man inwards to his heart. They do not target one's garments. They target flesh and work their way inwards to the body's core, where they gather like maggots and create a hollow of intense heat like a furnace. The blackened rags, previously worn by Michael's body, were the result of ordinary fire, which, although every bit as effective as the fire of a preta, is certainly more easily quenched.

'You will not escape from this place *alone*,' the penetrating voice of the deceased monk returned, and seemed to emanate from every direction, so that Michael spun in search of him.

'Where are you?' Michael asked, 'it cannot be! I saw you accidentally perish in the experiment of your making! Even your spirit should be destroyed!'

The monk chuckled very loudly at Michael's misassumptions and said, 'I am wherever you *want* me to be.' When Michael turned towards the church's door, he was greeted by the very image of the monk as he had known him before, with his eyes hidden by his hood, and the hitherto bitter line of his mouth contained a nuance of accomplishment. In confusion and dread at the powers of the monk, Michael started back towards the location on the floor where he had watched the heretic incinerate, just moments earlier.

'As you may have gathered, unlike a lot of people, I am no mere lump of flesh to be stabbed or burned. What you are looking at is not a person. In fact, you're the only one here who can sense me. I want you to listen very carefully to my explanation of what just happened here.' Immediately, Michael felt the immense wisdom of the monk, and was overcome by the need to pay close attention to the words of Guidonis, in spite of the maintained horror and uncertainty of the whole scenario. He listened to every word with great care, as the heretic began to account for how his life was saved, for what purpose, and at what cost. Michael knew that it would be impossible to run, and impossible to escape his fate, for the monk's spirit had been fused with his body by the twisted science in the church, and it would follow him wherever he went.

'Your soul is now in a coalition with two others,' the monk began, 'I am one of those souls. The other is your sister, Berenice. She will answer your call, or come to your aid, and may appear before you, as I do.

47

Although your spirit is exclusively in control of this body and its physical activities, the other two souls also inhabit your body. It is in our collective interests to ensure that your quest is successful. And we will be able to aid you in ways that you cannot possibly begin to imagine. You know your quest already. Your quest is already embedded in you, the seeds of vengeance. What is it that you wish to do, Michael? What will you use your restored body to do?'

'I must return to battle against Hydra! I must stop them! I don't want to do anything else.'

'But you do! Think more specifically. What can you do to deliver the killing blow that will destroy Hydra?'

'Hardrad must be killed! I must destroy him at any cost!' Michael exploded in vengeful fury.

'This is necessary. It is not simply your vengeful desire. If you don't, then Rose will be reduced to ashes, just as your body would otherwise have been. If you are prepared to turn this defeat around, to exorcise evil from the nations of mankind, just as I have exorcised the pretas from your flesh now, then nothing can stand in your way. You will cut through to the heart of the Hydra. You will destroy Hardrad and his lieutenants utterly, and his realm will be ended.'

'How is a deed of such immeasurable valour and physical strength possible?'

'Do not question. Begin your quest right away. You have been given your task, and you must see it through to completion. No time for questioning. No time for hesitation. No time for mercy. You must do dark deeds, and it will be the last battle of good and evil. Hardrad will drown in his own blood, and Hydra will be undone. This quest is to be treated as a necessary evil that you must endure, for the survival of Rose. If not, for the *world*. There is only one primary peril that I need warn you of, now. It is the most important thing I need you to keep in mind, at all times throughout the quest. This process of healing, although giving you certain abilities beyond any mortal man, has unleashed entities that were once spiritual constituents of the darkest parts of your character. Your own mortal mind contained the most terrifying creature imaginable, kept safely within the prison of the living body, suppressed by the soul, and it is there to perform the harvest of the soul when it reaches death, but yours has been dislocated, for you are neither living nor dead. And you have never faced such creatures before. The embodiments of doubt and fear will come as demons

49

and seek to lead you astray, so that the quest fails, and the world falls. You will be haunted by them throughout your quest. The conflict is not ultimately between you and Hydra. It is a conflict within you. A battle you must win.'

And, as if she had emerged from the solid stone of the enclosure, as easily as passing through air, Berenice came and was present in the church with him, to inform him, 'father continues to believe that you were dishonourable in the attack on the village. He won't forgive you. Only a deed of the greatest valour with your newly healed body could persuade him to forgive your.'

'How can I change that?' Michael begged, surprised at such stubbornness, even from his father. It seemed absurd that one should persist in worldly ignorance, even after death, but it came upon Michael that such is indeed the cause of much restlessness among the dead, that leads them to haunt the places of the living.

'There is only one way our father will forgive you. You must bring death to Kraide and then to the other lieutenants of Hardrad, as the monk has bid you. Destroy them, and you will atone for your dishonour.'

'How can you assist me?'

'We are not sure of that, ourselves. Even I am not sure,' Guidonis resumed, 'until you combat our enemy, we cannot promise the exact manner in which you will triumph over death. But, I warn you, physical pain will still be real for you, although you will be shielded from death. I cannot explain exactly how this works. And, although you are less vulnerable to corporeal defeat, you are now more vulnerable to spiritual harms. We rely our power as three. Three spirits, working together for the maintenance and success of one body. With our combined skills, and our equal commitment to our mission, the quest may be accomplished. But you are the central being in this, Michael. Everything depends on you. Do we have your consent?'

'I give my fullest devotion to this quest. I will have no other thought, henceforth. But no-one knows the map and the nature of Hydra's mysterious lands. No-one understands them, or has ever ventured into their perilous lands. I do not know where to begin. I do not know what I will find,' Michael told the sorcerer.

'You must travel to the various bastions of Hydra, one by one. There, you will find Sephric lords. You must kill each of them, and any of their servants in your path who seek to stop you. But the Sephrics will be formidable opponents. I cannot guarantee that we will be successful, unless we maintain the fullest devotion to the quest. There will be nothing that may occupy your mind, now. Only the mission to kill Hardrad. And to destroy Hardrad's line. Hardrad and his son Draco must be killed. It is necessary, so he may have no successors,' Guidonis instructed.

'I know nothing of the Sephrics or their wicked sorcery, so I have no way to confront them,' Michael said, 'I must know more, before I depart and attempt to fulfil the quest.'

'I know all that you need to know, and there is no need for an inquisition on all things, right now,' Guidonis said, 'I'm not going to abandon you. I'm connected to your corporeal form, as is your sister. Remember this. I am always here to guide you. I will appear at your bidding and help you. Nonetheless, you are wise to ask for a deeper understanding of the Sephrics, before seeking to combat them. You know nothing of their nature beyond the evil that they have wreaked, thus far, against the Rose. What I am going to tell you is everything I know about their mysterious origins.

'Know that Hydra has not merely devastated these lands. They have devastated many. They do not enslave. They do not even interact in a human fashion with other nations. They only kill, as if their country is a wild animal, driven by a belief the whole world should be its territory. Driven by greed. Driven by one motive. Their ability to take whatever they wish and destroy whoever they wish. It can destroy and consume other nations, so why should it not? Responsibility and moral obligation is irrelevant to he who possesses unchecked power and is surrounded by nations of sheep, who hold them only with terror. Nations that know nothing of them, and possess no way of threatening them back. Not even a single attempt has been made to understand their language, because they have never sought to engage in dialogue. In fact, the only moments when we have ever the evil tongue of Hydra, in Rose, have been the moments when they were uttering black curses and military commands during their campaigns against the innocents of the world. And you will never negotiate with them. The Hydrans know only war. They are beyond redemption. They have tied their fate to that of their war. And their war must be ended, in a relentless campaign of destruction, or the whole world will come to destruction. The Sephrics must perish, and it must be done as hard and as fast as possible. They will not ask for forgiveness, because they provide none. Their only regret will be that their war was lost. Their last dying thought will be only of killing you. They are more interested in the satiation of their desire for conquest than the luxury of being alive. To be rid of them is an act of mercy on the world, and execution is the only possible act of compassion towards the Hydrans themselves.

'No-one knows of their origins. There is no historical chronicle that can tell us what happened before the Sephrics were among mankind. But I can show you what they are, so that you will know your enemy. Close your eyes, and you will *see* the answer to your questions on the nature of Hydra. During this vision, you will perceive what I observed of the Sephrics, when I was in the deathly sleep that only comes upon the psychic explorers who ingest the water of the Styx. What you discover may be disturbing, and you may terminate this vision, at any point, if you feel that you are experiencing spiritual damage in the process. Do you wish to proceed?'

'Yes. I must see, so that I can know what my enemies are,' Michael decided, and the three of them closed their eyes and formed a circle, holding hands, and they began a journey of the mind's eye, into the past visions of the sorcery of Guidonis.

Two demons in the guise of serpents emerged among the rocks at the Volcano of the North, and they slithered their way south, until they came to a small village. Here, they found a boy and a girl, undefended by their parents, so they converted back into their demon forms and possessed them.

The boy and girl then went about doing mischievous and wicked things, and they killed their families and struck terror into the village, so that the villagers drove them out. They then lived as wretches in the mountains, by the volcano from whence they had originated, until they were old enough to command the dark powers to put a curse on the village. At this point, they returned. They put a spell on the village and the bodies of the villagers were placed under the command of demons, and the evil man and woman ruled over the village.

The evil man and woman bred, producing demon sons and daughters. They were strong-willed, with an unrivalled capability to govern, and the sinister light shining from their eyes struck terror into all the humans who were unaffected by their sorcery. They never exhibited any sign of weakness, physical or mental, and they seemed only to be rivalled by others of themselves, ruthlessly competing for power within their own realm, unafraid of murdering one another to claim the highest reachable office of king. They spent all their time teaching their evil children the same powers of sorcery, that they had commanded, and they went about repeating the process of the takeover on other villages. Eventually, the creatures became the royalty of a nation of sleepless cursed warrior-slaves. And they forced this irredeemable population to serve and worship them. The evil king ruled his tyrannical nation from the great fortified city that stood where their village once was. Their plan was for their offspring to be as numerous as the stars in the sky, and to force mankind to forever nurture them, as slaves. From this moment forward, no-one came forward to oppose them. They feared no hand other than their own power-hungry relatives, because the Sephric way of succession was only by killing one's superior.'

The vision made Michael certain that he must end the Sephric madness; that he must arise as their assassin. The road was ready for him, and he knew what he had to do.

'I am ready to embark on this quest,' Michael said, 'show me the way to Hydra's gates.'

'I will guide you, every step of the way.'

III. THE BATTLE OF THREE STAIRS

Michael's mind's eye had experienced a vision of the sickening origins of the rotten Hydran enemy, and this had formed the foundations of his new mercilessness towards them, so that he had no regard for their human forms. Because their inhuman evil was undeniable before him, he chose to see them and all their servants as true monsters. He would not be capable of compassion towards them or anyone who chose to side with them, even if they should repent. The soldiers of Hydra were the puppets of demons, inhabited by tortured and vengeful entities that were driving them to untold levels of cruelty. They knew of their own wickedness, and their only purpose was to destroy whatever they saw to be good in the world. They existed to maliciously spoil whatever majesty or light crossed their path, because their knowledge of it bred their hatred of it. They would ravage all things and drive this world into darkness and misery, so that all other beings might become like themselves. In his devotion to stop them, Michael could not afford conscience or humanity to stay his hand. It was incumbent upon him to purge all evil from the world. To slay the Sephric parodies of humanity. To say that Michael risked his sanity, in committing to such a dark ambition as to shed every drop of their evil blood, would be valid only if he had retained any degree of it after the Sephrics had educated him in the true nature of war. Through Guidonis, he had been granted the terrible knowledge of what the enemy planned for the world. Ash and blood would be the foundations of their empire. Such an outcome was unacceptable! If there had to be ash, blood and bones, it would have to be found in Hydra's own ruin. Hydra's own fate would correspond with the vision of Hell that they had planned for the world. Hardrad, in death, would know consequences of his war.

Through Guidonis's great capability to sense the actions of the enemy from afar, Michael became aware of the Hydran attack on the sacred Three Stairs, and the Rose raids of retaliation that had been launched against the Hydran occupiers' camp, only to meet their certain doom. Now, the Rose raids had intensified, and the Hydrans had consolidated their forces into a defensive strongpoint on a ridge overlooking a plain beside the Three Stairs. The Rose had established their main camp on the mountainside and they were planning to attack the ridge. They were stubborn, for they believed that it was a crime not to act while the enemy desecrated one of the Constructor's holiest sites. At sunrise, the Rose would form up, ten thousand strong, on the plain before the ridge.

"We will form our forces into a crescent shape on the ridge," Prince Valdemar had explained to his bands of fighters, "and when I give the order, we will launch a central wedge attack toward the ridge. We aim to climb it and penetrate the heart of their formation. Our target is their leader, Lord Kraide. We must take his life, as a warning to the Sephrics that we are capable of killing more than just their beasts and slaves. Furthermore, without Kraide, they will break. Only through the brutal leadership of this entity is the demon horde kept intact. In the event that we find the effort in the centre fails, we will use both spikes of the crescent to encircle the enemy position and work inward on them from all directions. The enemy is consolidated on the ridge, but he is fewer than us. We must act quickly, before substantial Hydran reinforcements arrive.

"In the event that we achieve little success, overall, we will taunt the enemy and invite him with us as we eject forces into the pass on our left flank. This will be our emergency plan of retreat. We will evacuate into the pass and take up ambush positions on the sides of our path of ejection, to perform a rearguard action. Archers will harass the enemy from among the rocks. We have already made fortified positions in the pass, to make this possible. As we feign retreat, we will follow the pass around this very mountain, to the point where it accesses the ridge at the Hydran formation's present right flank. There, we will meet little resistance, because the Hydrans will have left that position to pursue us in the previous phase of the battle, and will be bogged down in the pass. With this advantage, we will usurp the Hydran position on the ridge, and charge down it to find our pursuing enemy's exposed flank. Then, we can get the soft part of the enemy formation rather than having to face their spearhead head-on. By that point, the enemy will have sustained substantial losses, his forces will be scattered, as will ours, and we will then have no other task than to hunt down the stragglers and stage ambushes. That will be easy, because we are all well-experienced in such an art, and considerably more so than we are in open-field warfare.

"You have all been informed of the battle plan. I expect you to conduct yourselves in as close accord with it as the situation in the field tomorrow shall permit. Now get some sleep. You will need all your strength and sharpness with you tomorrow."

On the day of the Battle at the Three Stairs, Michael joined with the Rose formation by blending among a band of grim militiamen as they were incorporated into the formation. There was little to no exchange of words between the soldiers as they looked to the Hydran positions on the ridge, where dark contingents of armoured infantry were observed forming up. A storm was being called in by the Hydran magicians. The sky was darkening and a terrible cloud was present above the plain. As they gazed out at the

Hydran formations, they could see ghostly white streams of lethal energy being fed, from the enemy positions, into the clouds. These were the channels that allowed the sorcerers to feed sinister energy into the sky, and it would later be emptied in a devastating display of supernatural, heretical power. But the Rose leader knew the power of such a storm, and had planned to minimise his army's exposure to it. Utilising the terrain had always been instrumental in achieving any degree of Rose combat success, whether they fought from concealment or in the open field, so Valdemar had made sure that the rugged terrain and the mountains were both essential components of his plan.

It was difficult for Michael to perceive the size of the Rose host, because he was enclosed within their formation, and was probably twenty ranks deep. The ranks were not uncomfortably close together, as they had been instructed to space out, two paces apart or so. To stand in a single clump would not only have made fifteen thousand men look less from afar, but it would also have proven dangerous in the event that the leaders lost control of the common soldiery and they rushed back and forth in tremulous confusion, crushing one another. The Hydrans, it had always been observed, had no such concerns for the safe coordination of their infantrymen, nor did they need it, because the excessive application of black magic was such that

Hydran soldiers were no more than mindless servants for their distant masters, and could have no fear of their enemies or the horror of war. Their fear of the whips of their own masters would ever be greater than their fear of the spears of the enemy.

And so it was, under the restless, unnatural crimson and black clouds, that General Valdemar ordered his central wedge formation to form, from the frontal rank of the crescent, and it began to traverse the plain towards the foot of the ridge. As it all commenced, Michael could see nothing of it, for he was concealed behind the ranks. But a chill passed through him, telling him that someone had blundered, and that the battle would surely be lost. History had always favoured Hydra in the open field, and the Rose had always fled, while those of them with courage were later mistaken for fools, left behind to their deaths. There was an instant, in those moments of ominous silence, when Michael felt certain that Guidonis was in the line, at his side, and that the heretic warned him, 'disaster is coming. You will not avail the armies of Rose.'

Michael heeded this, and came to believe that, most likely, the warning words of Guidonis were right. If the battle played out in accordance with the flawed plans of the leaders and the mortality of the soldiers, this would be the hour of doom for his country's army. He was ready to die for Rose, if only to gain his father's forgiveness and demonstrate his commitment to avenge his beloved sister's slaughter. But there was surely a greater reason for his presence on the field of battle on that day. He had been called here, because things essential to his destiny would come to pass here. There was a terrible significance to the battle, and he feared it, but he knew that it was his duty to do his part in the fighting, and to kill as many enemies as he might be able. He was not merely one mortal soul, who could be slain by one arrow, anymore. He was aided by two other beings. And their sacrificial power, he thought, might make him the secret Rose weapon in the battle, capable of turning the tide.

Guidonis delivered a disturbing revelation, when he told Michael, 'do not, as you are about to, feel ashamed that you did not participate in the present assault by the infantry wedge against the ridge. They are to perish. It is already done.'

His words had barely ended, when a white bolt of energy came down from the spiralling clouds of black and crimson, accompanied by a sound that the whole army would surely take to be the hammer of the Undergrave, and was succeeded by the screams of men dying, young and old, under the tormenting laughter of demoniac disembodied intelligences.

This was no ordinary battle. The battle was to be incapable of proceeding in accord with the expectations the men of Rose had of their Hydran foes, even after a hundred years of war against that army of conjurers and the risen dead. One could not expect these sights and sounds, even in battle with the warriors of the wicked king Hardrad, who led his army from afar with the most formidable of serpentine tenacity and malice, in his determination to prove his worthiness as the mightiest agent of the doom of mankind.

Although Valdemar's own confidence was surely shaken at the sight of his opening move's debacle, he was assuring his lieutenants that the reward of victory would still be attainable if they remained steadfast and adhered to the battle plan. He retained his confidence that the mountain pass would preserve most of the army, if all things should go awry in the field. All the soldiers were prepared to follow the commands of their chieftains, and all the chieftains knew and agreed with the tactical plan devised by Valdemar. Even if the plan was in error, nothing was more valuable at this time than coherent direction and organisation. Should dissent arise, and confidence in the leader of the Rose army vanish among his soldiers, then only the worst of outcomes would be witnessed on that day. The failure of the first attack was anticipated by many, and the Rose plan was not dependent on its success. But to see soldiers struck down by the power of the storm above, before they could even reach the obvious point of conventional vulnerability at the foot of the ridge, cast serious doubt on the assumption that this was a battle between mortal men at all. Michael and Guidonis both knew mortal men cannot hope to stand against such all-mocking and unassailable powers as there existed in Hardrad's hands.

After the failure of the opening advance, the entire Rose formation was directed to move fifty paces ahead. This had not been planned during the meeting prior to the battle, but Valdemar's lieutenants did not question the order, for they trusted their general's instincts. It was a sudden move by Valdemar, most likely twofold in its intent, for it intended on making his formation closer so that it could faster enact his next gambit, and it also sought to feign a full frontal assault, to alter the tactical arrangement of Kraide's forces. The former was the most obvious objective, because the Rose quickly stretched their forces into a much wider formation and approached the ridge in such a way that even Michael, from his concealed place amidst the lines, could tell that a double envelopment of the enemy position was the present goal.

The manner in which Valdemar's forces had moved across the field was foolish, and Michael suspected as much even without being cognizant of the battle plan. The premature realignment of the formation to facilitate an obvious pincer action exposed the Rose general's objectives to the Hydrans, and gave Kraide the luxury of substantial minutes to prepare a way of turning the Rose move into a disaster, before it could inflict any harm on his own position. Rose infantry were marching fearlessly towards the ridge, in such a way that Kraide's defence of the elevation might be difficult, because it would require precisely equal defensive force on every part of the perimeter, lest the ring burst at a perforation in the line of defence, and the whole ridge fall into Rose hands.

Kraide could certainly not risk endangering his position on the ridge to this foolhardy Rose advance, and was ready to call on his feared cavalry forces. So, as the Rose soldiers reached the foot of the ridge, undetered by the skies, even as the enchanted lightning continued to strike them, the advancing infantry prepared to ascend. And then Kraide revealed the deadly secret that had been essential to his own battle plan. He had been concealing a vast sum of war demons behind the ridge, and the Rose had now reached a convenient state of vulnerability. With inadequate reconnaissance provided by the largely inexperienced army of Rose peasants, Valdemar had advanced blindly. He had taken to the offensive while he possessed no knowledge of what lay behind the ridge.

As the Rose formation attempted to curl its way around the ridge's right side, not just a hail of poisoned arrows descended upon them. The concealed cavalry force of dragons, titans and armoured serpents intercepted the Rose lines at their right flank and drove through them at this point of exposure, where they were narrow and possessed too few pikes to establish a barrier of defence against the beasts. The stampeding reptiles of Hydra roamed free of their chains. And, like giant maces, they smashed all the shields, spears, swords and skulls before them. The significant numbers of the Rose infantry were useless, and they were at the mercy of the demons, so they were rapidly ridden down like grass. The Rose battle horns immediately signalled the emergency plan of withdrawal, but the formation took this as permission for their terrified flight back in a shambles towards the pass. None of the pike-carrying militiamen retained any demeanour of strength or confidence at that point. They fled like a broken rabble of children. Only the experienced archers and rangers seemed to have any resolve. With their bows and spears, the archers and rangers did succeed in bringing down several of the mighty war demons, before Valdemar commanded those bravest of his soldiers into the pass to accompany his fleeing army.

The war demons were recalled by Kraide, because they were now spread too thin, and several had been slain near the mouth of the pass, which appeared to be filled with bands of Rose guerrillas, stationed there to mount a rearguard action. But Kraide did not fear the Rose rearguard, and his withdrawal of his cavalry did not mean he abandoned his gleeful desire to pursue what he saw as a fleeing flock of sheep. Nor did he wish to abandon his opportunity to claim Hydra's greatest southern victory as his own. He wished to send a substantial amount of infantry to assist the reptilian war beasts as they pursued the Rose through the pass. To that end, he quickly prepared his horde for such an advance, but left the royal soldiers of Hardrad in reserve, on the ridge. This, it seems, was the only detail of the battle predicted by the much shaken General Valdemar.

The mounted war demons, that had sought to violently pervade the Rose formation at their right. had certainly been the most unpleasant surprise of the battle. But there were also several further strikes of lightning from the whirling black clouds against the fleeing Rose forces on the grey plain. As the final soldiers fled from the open plain, they were tormented by yet another weapon of the tortured sky, and it was a device of such horror that Kraide's own pursuing forces went around the plain's centre as they tried to reach the mouth of the pass, lest they share in its torments.

Now Michael was caught in the wrath of this pernicious weapon of Hydran magic. He was limping towards the safety of the pass, at this time, because the filthy tooth of a small species of dragon had impaled his leg and remained there in his flesh, dealing some kind of terrible curse against him. He had cut through the dragon's neck when it attempted to devour him, but its Hydran forked tongue had contaminated his wound and his body was once again being flooded with demoniac influences. Finally, that next pernicious weapon of the enemy came. And Michael succumbed to the evil power within the black cloud above him when a downpour of acid came and burned his flesh, until the bodies of he and his fallen comrades alike were utterly reduced to pools of blood and contorted bone. It was a terrible and ugly battlefield, soaked black with death. Valdemar's extraction through the pass might have prevented the rout of the Rose army being complete, but the battle seemed over for the liquefied remains of Michael. His soul floated in darkness, its body broken.

It was some hour later when, aided by the miraculous powers of Guidonis, Michael rose again. His flesh was certainly scarred, but the benevolent magic of Guidonis was reshaping him and wiping those scars away, reconstructing his dissolved organs and bone. The process was painful, like death running in reverse, or perhaps like the introduction of a baby first exposed to the cold of the air. But, after minutes of gore and agony, writhing on the dark-stained plain, Michael rose again. The bones of his hands, which had previously been exposed by the acid, were concealed beneath flesh and skin once more. He took some mail and armour from nearby, and clothed himself for his return into combat.

Now, as he observed the battlefield and his sight returned, he saw that it was still dark, and the storm still rumbled restlessly above him, but its bombardment of the earth with bright bolts of lightning and spilled acid had lapsed, to allow the Hydrans to move across the plain. Now, as he crawled among the molten dead, he could see the unclear shapes of the snarling Hydran war demons, moving into the pass, and a stream of pike men carrying the black Hydran banner accompanied them. Again, Michael's vision faded. All was blurred for a few seconds, and then he saw movement nearby, so he stayed motionless, lest he draw the attention of a Hydran soldier.

As he regained the ability to see clearly, he discerned a titanic figure. There stood a dark-caped lord of Hydra, so giant of frame that his footsteps made the battlefield shake. The lord came close, and, observing the liquefied remains of his foes, looked down upon the body of Michael. And Michael's eyes met those of the Hydran lord, and in that moment he knew that he had found the guilty one. A deathly pale visage of a bony shape, the sinister glow of the eyes, and the blackness of his beard, were all features proving his identity was Kraide of the House of Sephric. Michael knew this appearance belonged to the very same lord responsible for the destruction of Loom and the death of Berenice. So, knowing he had found his moment of atonement at last, Michael rose from the black decay of the battlefield to fight the general.

The armoured titan exclaimed something in the Hydran language, in the very same mocking voice Michael had witnessed at Loom. Although unable to understand his enemy's babble, Michael knew the anger in the voice, and the Sephric's mere presence commanded a terrible aura of power and dark otherworldly wisdom. He was much taller than Michael, and stood over him like his immortal master.

Michael now most certainly recognised the evil light in his enemy's eyes, and knew the general carried the evil blood of the Sephric House in his veins. The inhumanly pale complexion and the darkness of the beard were unmistakeable, as well as the bony visage and the greed contained within the icy serpent eyes. This was surely the same lord of barbarians responsible for all the evil that was unleashed upon the village, and the same one who had dealt such terrible injuries against Michael's flesh. Now, he would reap the product of his evil deed, and know the terrible pain and darkness that he had so long professed in unleashing on others.

They battled each another for many hours in fierce personal combat, and Kraide did not seem alarmed or deterred by Michael's extraordinary resilience. In fact, by the look contained in his sadistic eyes, he appeared to be entertained because he had finally encountered one shepherd after so many years in combat with mere sheep. The manner in which Kraide fought was informative, and told Michael that the general had already experienced enemies of similar tenacious resistance and durability before.

By his forked tongue, the Sephric used his occult knowledge to call upon the clouds, so that they delivered lightning to his aid against the seemingly indestructible soldier. When this was ineffective, his fanged expression turned to frustration, because he had discovered that his own greatest skills were valueless against the strange healing abilities of Michael. He uttered a curse that turned his sword white with heat, and it succeeded in melting through Michael's armour. But, as it passed into the risen soldier's flesh, its path was stopped by the resilience of the enchanted body, and the wound healed, even as the sword continued to occupy the deep place it had cut through to. Kraide's blade was also drained of its heat, and Michael's flesh only healed faster, as if it drew away the enchantments and added them to its own, to increase its own survival. So Kraide furiously pulled the blade from his foe's chest, and took to striking Michael repeatedly at the same limb, in hopes of cutting off his fighting right arm. But Michael only learned from that course and imitated him, by repeatedly striking the Sephric's own right arm. By this wise action, the Sephric's armour was breached, and his bleeding arm was finally severed.

Michael's heart accelerated as his eyes beheld the dark Sephric blood gushing out onto the deathly grey plain, devoured by the soil. In fascination, Michael half expected the severed limb to burst into flames as the Undergrave reclaimed its property, but no such event occurred. The Sephric bodies were, evidently, extraordinarily resilient human bodies, through the aid of sorcery, possessed by hellish influences. But the flesh, itself, was evidently human in origin, just as Michael's own. Still, the chilling discovery of the human interior of the Sephric did not prevent his utter contempt for the relentless barbarian. And Kraide continued to attack him as no mortal man would, even with his arm reduced to a bloody stump.

Although Kraide's arm had been severed, and his dark end seemed surely near, the general did not fail to utilise one more unholy weapon. He uttered a curse that distorted Michael's perceptions of time and motion. All things immediately assumed a state of visual and auditory flux. He thought gravity itself had altered, so that he would fall towards a restless dark sky, now seemingly whirling below him. This strange sensation only lasted several seconds, but, in the brief moment of blurred imagery and disorientation, he discerned an axe-head being delivered toward his neck by the remaining hand of the deadly Hydran warrior. A glowing, pale shape projected from him, and Michael saw that it was the arm of his own saintly sister Berenice. Her celestial being was reaching out to protect her brother. Her hand, although so slender that the mighty Kraide could twist it off with barely the use of a finger, stopped the evil general's hand with righteous force. And, now, persuaded by this evidence of his quest's infallibility, Michael snatched the axe from his adversary's hand, and used it to cut the muscular legs from beneath the Sephric general. And the body of Kraide collapsed into the dark pool of his own blood on the plain, his death fast approaching.

The general's body was broken, and Michael regarded the rotten sight of the twitching remains of the fallen leader of Hydra's war. This bleeding thorax, equipped with only a head and a quaking left arm, was crawling along away from him, as if trying to escape the expanding dark of its own blood leaking onto the plain. The hissing, the shaking forked tongue, the exposed fangs, and the void of the bloodied mouth, all confirmed the demoniac interior beneath the human appearance. Because he was committed to his quest, in all its unsightly duties, Michael finished his part in the battle, by hacking off the remaining limb in a display that could match the worst butchery of the whole war. In amazement at the ease of his deed, Michael looked down on the hewn torso of Kraide, and its vicious face. Blood continued to spill from the wounds, the dark pool expanding around it on the grey plain.

But, as Michael turned away from the hideous sight, he heard the sound of hissing behind him, and a mass of serpents descended on him. The body of Kraide had risen again, this time with great serpents projected from each stump of its severed limbs. Altogether, there were seven serpents. Four of them became limbs and propelled the horrible tower of Kraide's mighty thorax and fiery-eyed head towards the assassin. The stumps of his arms had released another three serpents, which plunged at Michael and tore at his flesh.

As Michael backed away in horror at his discovery of the truth of Sephric inhumanity, one of the snakes was too quick. It succeeded in rapidly encircling him, lifting him into the air by his waist, and he was brought closer to the expanding mouth of Kraide. As the fangs reached him, they dug into his neck, and the serpents all tightened around each of his arms. But, the tighter the grip of the snakes became, the stronger Michael's own arms became in resisting them.

When Michael had mustered enough of his enchanted might, he kicked and slashed with his sword. And, with great valour, he broke free of the seven snakes, and they recoiled in fear at his fury. Now he approached the beast to make his own attack, and all the seven heads rose and then dived down at him in protection of the torso of Kraide. Michael slashed them back with his sword, and severed the head of one assailing serpent. Blood flowed from the fallen snake, and the other six plunged aggressively upon the warrior once more. When he slashed again relentlessly with his blade in fury, Michael successfully dismembered half of the remaining creatures from the bloody torso of the lord. Seeing that his end was near, the remaining snakes tried to drag the erect torso of Kraide away from his assassin, and the lord's psychic mind communicated to his army, so they might all converge onto the place of his vulnerability and save him. There was a rumbling of the approach of fierce demonic cavalry, abandoning their pursuit of the Rose in the pass, to defend their lord, but they were too late.

Michael pursued the beast, and hacked away the last three serpentine projections in his eagerness to complete his vengeance, so that only the upright torso remained, armour fallen away to expose a blood-splattered white mass, the eyes of the skull burning like fiery pits. Finally, the defeated body fell into the pool of its own blood, and Michael stood over the ruin of Kraide. To be sure that the creature was dead, Michael cut through the mighty neck of the Sephric, and Kraide's head came down and rolled over in the pool of his own blood, his forked tongue emerging and licking the dark pool. Michael looked down on the massive head of his grotesque malefactor, and watched the fire fade from the eyes of the wicked lord, until he was sure that Kraide was dead. Michael had believed he would feel the completion of his vengeance, but the feeling did not come. It was not yet complete.

In his fury, and his knowledge of his mission of vengeance, Michael proceeded to cut out the forked tongue and slash the Sephric lord's eyes in their dark pits in an intolerably disgusting ritual, brought about by the manipulative influences of Guidonis upon his actions. He then impaled the hideous skull on a spear, and the planted this pike into the soil. It served as a terrible warning sign for Hydra to back away from these lands. But Michael knew the Hydrans would only be infuriated by it, and would double their efforts against their southern opponents. Michael would be forced to repeat this act of deterrence many times. And Hardrad's war would only end with his own death.

The remainder of the battle saw the rout of the Hydrans, because the loss of their commander sent them running in fear and confusion, and Michael cut many of them down, even as he departed from the battlefield. The remaining Hydran forces, including their terrible war demons, were all cleansed from the area during the Rose search for stragglers that ensued. None were spared, for the Rose wished to deter the Hydrans from ever returning. The soldiers sent by Hardrad to assist his general were leaderless, and they fled in the most cowardly manner into the wilderness, until each of them was found and killed, and their black banners were all captured and burned.

In their celebrations, the Rose dragged all of the black serpent banners onto the plain and burned them, along with the heaped remains of Kraide and his soldiers. The Rose people made a great display of the body of Kraide, for they had now discovered the monstrous nature of the Sephrics. They mocked Hardrad. They called him a coward, who had never left the confines of the chambers of his fortress, and would now witness the end of all his armies and perish with the last remnants of his realm in those chambers. The battle had witnessed the destruction of his finest battalions at the hands of peasants.

It would take months for the Hydrans to rebuild a new southern army with the manpower to mount a reinvasion under new leadership. But the victory was not accredited to General Valdemar, whose tactical errors in the battle were all too obvious. Instead, it was attributed to the mysterious and valorous act of the assassination of the Sephric general, as occurred on the battlefield, and no-one learned who was responsible, although there were whispers that only the feared Order of Transpathy could have been responsible. That day, begun as one of terrible misfortune for Rose, had quickly turned into their greatest victory, which would be recorded as the turning point in the conflict, when evil met its match. The armies of Hydra had fallen, and Hardrad remained concealed in his castle, a coward.

As he walked away from the battlefield, Michael thought about the disturbing nature of his enchanted body, and the manner in which his corpse had healed and reawakened on the battlefield. For a moment, he had thought of rejoining his comrades and celebrating the victory that he had helped them to attain. But he was no longer mortal. He was not willing to go and join their celebrations, for it was not in accord with the quest. Guidonis counselled him, telling him that he was wise not to dwell among his countrymen anymore, for he was a cold instrument, and no mortal would understand the true importance of the quest. They would also be fearful of him, and he would risk the Rose taking him for a witch, which would lead them to become his enemy, and that would cause an unhappy fate for all those whose survival depended on the success of the quest. The quest depended on secrecy and speed, and Michael knew that his former countrymen would not understand. Joy was not a thing that he would never know again, and he accepted this. That way of life had been taken from him. He had to face the Sephrics alone. Their monstrous conflict, now, was with him alone.

Michael was fearful for what he had become, because he had perished and risen again, and slaughtered so many men in the battle. Something very strange, unnatural, and heretical had happened back there, in his endurance of the acid storm. The ways of the heretic Guidonis, meant manipulating Michael's very flesh. And so the first seeds of his doubt about the rightfulness of the quest were now sown in his heart. He feared how many times, more, he might need to perish and return, and what hideous spiritual fate might be waiting for him, if he should continue on this path of necessary self-destruction. He feared the judgment of his pained soul, and he both loved and hated the quest dominating him. It was a quest to achieve fell deeds of vengeance, and its fuels were anger and hatred. He could not suppress his desire to bring devastation upon those he hated, for he knew that nothing could oppose him, and so he feared his own power. He feared the deeds that he had proven himself capable of. His hatred of the Hydran rulers would drive him into committing countless more dark deeds, he knew, and his soul would continue to inhabit a body with unnatural resistance to rightful death. He would live, even though he had already earned his rightful death many times. The very continued existence of this body, this abomination, was an unforgivable act of heresy, yet the cause of its quest was still good.

IV. THE FORBIDDEN

The Grave Expanse, which was known by a less dark name, the White Forest, in a better period of history, rested along the southern edge of the Forbidden Mountains of the North. Back until time immemorial, the chronicles had always documented it as the terrifying boundary that separated Rose from the frozen wastes of the northernmost part of the world. And the Deathly Highway ran through the terrible expanse, a fearsome black mouth that invited doomed travellers through starved trees and their sinister shadows. Although that path was once left untrodden for centuries, the armies of Hydra had inevitably come thundering down it, for it was their primary marching route. But the trees had permitted a great sinister tunnel to allow travellers through it. It was as if the evil forces of the forest had sought to create a mouth with which they could devour the misled. Few chronicles had ever mentioned Rose travels into the region. In those chronicles that did portray the Deathly Highway, only unspeakable horror was found.

When he arrived on the Deathly Highway, he was a newly hooded and cloaked warrior, prepared as a traveller with a long road ahead of him and an errand of the utmost secrecy. Michael stood without fear of the Hydran armies he knew might easily come storming down it, and he would have proven eager to block their passage alone, no matter how great the enemy's numbers were. But, during the hours he stood silently in the howling northern winds before this dark passage into the Expanse, expectant of the coming foes, he was confronted by no adversary. So, in defiance of all the grave warnings about the horrors that might be contained within the Expanse, Michael entered in pursuit of his enemies, knowing that it might lead to the fulfilment of his quest for absoluteness of vengeance against Hardrad. He was the first man of Rose in centuries to set foot there, ready to brave the perils no other man of his realm had survived.

His silent venture down the shadowy tunnel of sinister vegetation was interrupted only by an intensification of the cold howling winds, and they now bore a chilling warning of the malicious icy intellects waiting at his distant destination, hungering for his destruction. Everything about the place was bidding him to turn away, but he would not succumb to his instincts. He was wary, but not deterred. Some peril greater than anything he had witnessed on the battlefield at the Three Stairs was present among the shadows that lay behind the many pale skeletal plants. The ghost of the forest was disturbed by his presence. Only armies of monsters had hitherto dared to pass. Yet one man now knew himself deadlier than them all, and he was determined to brave the perilous road alone, until he came into Hydra, where he would confront the Dark Realm's ruler Hardrad, and punish him for the evil he had unleashed on the world.

The creatures of the forest were hidden, silent with apprehension. There was something strange about this lone assassin, and no evil dared to hinder him as he passed through the shadows. He walked on, and dark came, and the moon stared coldly down at him, but it did not succeed in deterring him. All the omens of the man's doom, in his four days of walking without rest, went ignored, for his commitment to his quest's completion could never be undone.

At one time, a fearsome giant black dog dashed down the Highway among the shadows, and came upon the tireless wanderer in the moonlight. But when it looked at the assassin, it saw only the bitter and unrelenting expression in his clenched lips, and it could see no eyes, because of the shadow of his hood. Merely upon its discovery of the traveller's valour, a look of terror came into the creature's own flaming eyes. And it ran, yelping, back to its unnamed master afar. The travelling assassin was something far more unnatural than any raw demon wandering the earth, and he brought significant confusion and fear to the sinister entities inhabiting the already cursed and haunted forest, for he was the agent of his own evil, unlocked by the evils of others, in his quest to seek out Hardrad and educate him in the same unrelenting wickedness he had sought to monopolise.

Michael, the agent of vengeance with an insatiable thirst for the blood of darkness, knew he was nothing more than a weapon. He accepted his destiny as the deadly fragment of the sword of evil, but he was a fragment had broken off to pierce its own maker's heart. The spectral hand of Guidonis was maintaining Michael's body, and the sorcerer assured him that he would have the aid of unholy arts, enough to topple all that stood in his way. His sister's soul was always near, as his protector, within an astral space she possessed the keys to open and close the doors of. Michael did not pretend to understand the science of their wandering between worlds, but he could not deny that it was real, for his life was now dependent on it.

But, in spite of this terrible sacrificial alliance, in its unification of a martyred girl, an undying soldier and a heretical sorcerer, Michael still wept inside for his family's slaughter and the unhealing scars of his soul. Only the powers of Guidonis, he knew, were keeping him from turning against himself and abandoning his quest. As he wandered the darkness of the forest, Michael was soon lost among the skeletal trees and the ocean of his own consciousness. His soul was in great pain, fearful of being damned to spiritual annihilation, because he knew what a monstrous thing he had become through the heresy of Guidonis in preventing his mortal departure. And he knew a dark fate would be unavoidable if he carried these powers far enough for him to accomplish the quest. He would suffer cosmic torments because of his complicity in the unnatural heresies of Guidonis. These pains of the spirit, he knew, were the beginnings of an internal conflict that might become more dangerous to him than his battle against Hydra. To butcher the bodies of humanity, in the spirit of aggression rather than protectiveness, even if they were the instruments of demons, was still a path to the Abyss. This was a moral he had been raised with. His life had never prepared him for such a destructive form of martyrdom as confinement in eternal darkness so that he could know that he had achieved the salvation of his country and his loved ones' spirits. The Constructor of the universe was cruel to make him such a puppet.

So he asked his tutor, 'what will become of me, if I should proceed and turn myself over to evil practices, to save innocents?'

Upon hearing these doubts in the heart of Michael, the hooded spectre of Guidonis emerged from the shadows and acquired an appearance of reality as convincing as Michael's own substance, and said to him, 'turn yourself over to evil? You are deceived. You know nothing of the powers you speak of. You are foolish to ask this question, and that you should ask it is a cause for me to suppose a number of grave things about you. You have seen, for yourself, that you are incapable of death, so why do you fear death? You will never need to confront death if you remain in the bonds of this coalition. This is an everlasting alliance. You need not concern yourself with religious superstitions. What I have made use of is science, and I have perfected it to the highest degree. If you should fear it, like a child, then you will make the accomplishment of your quest less likely.'

'I want to be able to achieve redemption, to reclaim my honour, and end all of this meaningless butchery. I don't want to be a restless wanderer on the earth, the product of your wretched experiments. If I do have doubts about the righteousness of this quest, those doubts are wise indeed.'

'The forces of good are with you, because your cause is just. Think not of the physical appearance of the deeds the quest entails. Think only of the quest's end.'

'It is not glorious to slaughter the victims of evil. The Hydrans are but the victims of manipulative, evil personages. The Sephric are fallen beings, corrupted and tortured. All beings were once good. Perhaps I should not slaughter them. I am not unlike those victims.'

'You must proceed and complete this quest, or the events you witnessed at your home will repeat themselves a thousand times,' Guidonis said, and Michael's skin suddenly burned, as it had done before in the last moments of the village of Loom. 'I don't want to see your suffering. But you know our fates are shared. Our destinies are shared. Our objectives are mutual. And the only thing that stands between us and our victory over Hydra is your weakness. Your doubts are despicable! I thought you were strong, that you were the one to bring an end to this evil that has spread across the land. The undefeatable soldier is the one who can withstand any pain! Let the instruments of evil shatter when they touch this body! You need not fear lasting darkness or pain. If it must end in the Undergrave, and you fail to achieve spiritual redemption, then that outcome could never be more tolerable than it is now, for the fulfilment of the quest. I must have your commitment and determination. Let this burning of your skin be a taste of the pain that you will only find faster, and which will also be found by all the people of oppressed nations with you, if you do not go out and complete the quest for them! The spiritual fate of one person may be important, but it is insignificant compared with the temporal fate of the whole of mankind. Right now, we are discarding it.'

Michael fell to the ground in the reproduced agony he had experienced in Loom's destruction, and he descended into an ocean of boundless darkness, as if he had slipped and fallen into a chasm that he had not seen, that intersected the Highway. Plunging into the state of torment that Guidonis had readied for him, he felt trapped and alone, in some other plane of existence, where he would always be empty. His consciousness had been robbed away once more, as it had been during the heretical ritual in the church. Surely, Guidonis was demonstrating the capabilities that he would use to discipline this foolish body to serve him.

'What will this torture accomplish?' Michael asked, 'neither of us will achieve anything if I am gone now. You need me to go on this quest willingly!'

'Gone? Not at all. I am only educating you. There is a huge depth of knowledge that goes to the nexus of conflict between good and evil. And you are not welcome to gaze on it or to eat of that fruit, least you descend into irreparable insanity. It is too much. But you can at least be educated about the barrier itself. There is a barrier of darkness that you must not pass. The perfect but perilous esoteric knowledge of the scope of good and evil lies behind it. And that why you must not pass.'

'This is a deception! I am losing faith in you and your promises, Guidonis!'

'Listen! The impossibility of a deception should be obvious to you. A coalition of three souls imprisoned in one body cannot tolerate deception, so you are a fool to accuse me of it. There is no deception in this alliance other than *yours*, and I have brought you here to end it, because I have knowledge of your weakness.'

'I know your designs, and they contain heresies,' Michael retorted, 'I sense deceit in you. There is a hidden agenda. You are using me!' But he knew that his words were only sprung from his painful confusion, and they were unproductive. He was being insolent towards his master. He was divided. He needed discipline, or he would destroy what little purpose he still had. An individual can have great conflicts within, but there were three individuals guiding this body, and he had to contend with that greater capacity for internal turmoil. It was the drawback of the extraordinary corporeal healing abilities, as if, going into battle, he carried a double-edged sword.

'I require my sister's light and wisdom. She will judge you,' Michael demanded, and he was joined by her reassuring voice in the dark, but he could still see nothing. He did not believe that Guidonis bade her to come forth. She had answered to his call.

'You are being taken to a place of shadow and flame. It is not a good place to witness,' the voice of Berenice warned him.

'The Undergrave?' he responded in a quavering voice.

'No. But it is another place of torment, and it is a nest of evil, because it breeds the same entities that often escape and commit mischief in the world, and the same beings were responsible the demise of Loom.'

'Is there cause to suspect evil in the heretic Guidonis?'

'Guidonis is an enigma we do not comprehend. There is something beyond our comprehension in his designs.'

'Is this a reason to break the alliance?'

'Guidonis is the source. A heretic though he may be, and a man who uses many dark powers for his ends, he is the guardian of this quest, and this quest is good in its purpose. But the quest is yours alone, Michael. Do not deceive yourself that you have become a puppet. Guidonis selected you for the quest because you were prepared and willing. There is no perceivable deception and there is no puppetry. If he has evil ambitions, we will learn of them. And only then will it be wise to break the alliance.'

The heretic returned and silenced Berenice, just as her voice was going to start again, and he said, 'I warn you, Michael, that this woman's wisdom is limited. Your faith in your sister is foolish. She is a mere uneducated girl. She is here only to stabilise the coalition, because it was a ritual necessity to involve three. You cannot trust her for wise counsel.'

'I will not accept your pronouncement against her. I trust her with my life,' Michael defended, 'I cannot trust you, when you carry so much darkness with you. And you have brought me into this dark plane for torments, because I have not responded as a suitable slave. For these reasons, it is difficult for me to accept that your designs are as good as you claim.'

'Your consent is central to this alliance. Without you, the quest will fail. If one of us falters, and leaves this coalition, we will all be destroyed. Our fate will be terrible. Of this, I am prepared to educate you.'

Out of the Dark Realm he had occupied, Michael now opened his eyes to find himself imprisoned in a Hydran dungeon, with the sounds of screams echoing in the adjacent chambers, and he was hanging by his shackled wrists against a deathly cold stone surface beside the many bones and rotting carcasses of prisoners. He was unclothed and trapped in the dark. He was the only one alive in this chamber, although the other chambers still housed prisoners, where they were subjected to endless torments. Michael tried to rekindle the unnatural strength that he had known, so that he could attempt to break free of these shackles. He called upon his two spectral allies to aid him, but they did not answer. When he cried out for them, in his anguish and isolation, he only brought more agony and exhaustion to his hanging body. And he saw that only the soldiers of the enemy came and answered him. His inability to gather his previous strength and resilience was the result of an injury wreaked by the disunity of the coalition. He knew that it left him exposed to many evils.

The soldiers of the enemy came, and branded his forehead with a hot implement, which imprinted the seven-headed serpent seal of the Sephrics into the skin, and they subsequently cut his tongue from his grimace. As the dark blood poured from his jaw, he was reminded of the recent image of the assassinated General Kraide. If he was not prepared to commit these unsightly deeds against the enemy, as he did on the battlefield, he would witness all of that evil unleashed against the innocent. And he would still meet a dark end, regardless of his belief in the goodness of life and his craving for redemption. It was surely better to meet up with that fate of eternal fire whilst knowing that he had contributed to the security of his people, than to die in surrender and permit Hardrad to have his malevolent victory over the oppressed nations of the world. So, when the Hydrans proceeded to take his tortured body away and burn him at the stake under the whirling storm, he discovered that not only the unnatural resilience and magical protection of his body had faded, but his mortality had been fully restored and he would surely die.

'Michael, where is your drive for redemption? Are you reaffirming your cowardice?' his father's voice cried out to him from the sadistic chanting mob of undead warriors and wretched slaves who now encircled the pyre, 'by failing to retaliate, you have dishonoured me and there is nothing left for you.'

He groaned as his skin turned raw and melted, and his flesh bubbled, his veins haemorrhaging with the boiling content. And he saw the visions of many deaths. Deaths he could have suffered, yet risen again from the grave to take his revenge each time. And as he left the charred bones behind in the pyre, his spirit wandered back to his village of Loom. There, he studied the burning dwellings again, and witnessed the ravaged bodies of his kinsmen. So he descended, until he was occupying the same place amidst the devastation that had allowed him to see the perpetrator of the massacre and remember that evil visage until he killed the evil lord responsible. This moment had readied him, because it had educated him, by scarring his soul with unspeakable horrors. This was experience had given him the teaching preparing him for the unrelenting quest for vengeance and redemption. But the latter would remain outside his grasp, even when the former was accomplished, because it did not conform to the designs of Guidonis the heretic. In fact, because it is a universal law that fell deeds of vengeance shall not accomplish peace, it is certain that avengers cannot ever be redeemers. The desire for vengeance is an abyss. There is hungering wound, that craves vengeance, and it cannot be satiated. Eventually, the mouth of vengeance shall consume and destroy its own subject. It is a pit of destruction for everyone, and serves no purpose.

'There!' Kraide announced to his snarling soldiers who occupied the burning settlement, 'I have found one who presumes to survive!' And Michael, writhing in the pain of his renewed burns, was surprised to understand the words of the alien language. 'I smell fear and despicable weakness. Bring that roasted worthless body to me! It still has something in it! Something dangerous! We must silence him!'

So the soldiers lifted him from the fires and dragged him to the general, and Michael lay at the feet of Kraide. 'Do you not recognise the faces of the gods of this world?' the monster asked, 'you will worship us!'

'You are not my Constructor,' Michael choked, 'and I will show you all that you are made of less than flesh and blood. You are shapes of filth, unworthy of concealment anywhere except in the Undergrave.'

But laughter only erupted among the general and his soldiers, and Kraide said, 'you are nothing but a shape of meat to feed us, just like the body of your sister.' And he gestured to Berenice's unsightly remains, which were evidently being reduced to a skeletal remnant, fought over for the nourishment of Hardrad's soldiers.

'Cannibals?' Michael exclaimed, for he was both astonished and nauseous. He was enraged, and declared, 'so you have shown me that you are nothing but filth to be wiped from this world! You have declared war on humanity. What chance do you think you have? I am indestructible, even to all your sorcery. I will find and slay you all.'

'You are mistaken. We cannot die. No mortal man can annihilate us from this world. We are of an origin your tiny mind could never begin to imagine. This plane you call a world is nothing to us, for we know of spheres that are much better. This is but a stepping stone in our own neverending journey. Our armies have never fallen. Hydra knows no bounds, and we have the right to the ownership of this world. And now you will die a maggot's death. Prepare to learn the falsehood of your religion.'

'You are deceived,' Michael responded, and the rebellious flame in his eye made Kraide's blade stop, so that he could gloat and relish this particular kill. 'I won't die. None of this is real. It's an illusion, and you are nothing but a projection of my mind.'

'You know nothing of which you speak. Have you heard nothing that Guidonis, your master, has said?'

'What does the heretic mean to you? And why would you have any interest in aiding me by making me hear him?'

'Oh, I have done much to aid your master Guidonis. He is our instrument, and that is why he operates the powers that we gave him. Dark deeds are for dark ends. You could never have believed otherwise! In time, he will become suitably corrupted by these powers, and your coalition will alter its course, and serve us. We are the masters of these arts, and we only laugh at your presumption to use them back against us. You will become our weapon, and you will go back to slaughter our enemies for us, as our slave. Soon, you will destroy your own people. You will see the folly of your vain attempt to harm the House of Sephric.'

But, when the Sephric had finished delivering the revelation, a nearby warrior removed his hideous helmet and revealed that he was the heretic, spying on their exchange in the guise of a Hydran soldier. He said, 'Michael, do not listen to Kraide. He is lying. We killed him, and he knows that we can throw his House into the same abyss as he. That is why he wants you to terminate the coalition.'

And, as the Heretic continued to speak, in his attempts to draw Michael back to his enigmatic cause, Kraide turned on the sorcerer and growled, 'get back in rank, slave!' and cast him down onto a bloody track of mud among Loom's ruins.

'Why do you hesitate, Kraide?' Guidonis retaliated as he sprang back to his feet, 'are you fearful of the coalition? Is this why you feed doubt to Michael? How long have you gone about doing this? Have you clung to his presence since you fell at the Three Stairs, spectre? Your whole House is quaking in its knowledge of this resurrected soldier, because you have learned that your doom is at hand, and your conquests are over.'

'Kraide! He has been manipulating me from beyond the grave, all this time? All my doubts were sowed by this spectre?' Michael said in grief, as he tried to understand the crisis and determine his escape, 'I should have recognised the influence of a demon when I began to doubt the rightfulness of the quest. How could I have doubted my task? It was important that nothing be allowed to interrupt the quest, or the Sephrics will not suffer their correct punishment! This I decided as soon as I committed myself to quest inside the rock of the mountains of Rose.'

'And your quest is futile,' Kraide warned, 'we are all aware of you, and we know how to destroy your alliance. With each of us you kill, another such influence, as mine, will come and invade you! Your soul is fragile against us. In making your body impervious to mortal destruction, you made your soul more fragile, threefold.'

'Do not fear the lords of Hydra,' his sister's risen corpse said in the village, and Michael saw that it ceased to possess any injury but the fatal marks on the neck. The soldier was enthralled by the light in the words of Berenice, and he believed her. 'This is all nothing but a nightmare being projected by the tenacious lord Kraide to damage your devotion. All your doubts about the quest are the result of the spectre's influences. He is trying to pull you under, into the darkness of confusion in the forest of eternal loss.

Hold onto us and fight him, and you will stay in the benign presence of our light and knowledge. That is where you belong. Do not give him the chance to attack the coalition. Do not offer him any chance to damage or possess the body. A lapse such as this endangers us, because it suspends our power to protect the body, and leaves it vulnerable.'

There was the power of the sacrificial alliance protecting the body. Its disruption could be disastrous. There was a physical consequence that might leave him trapped in the dark fate. The maintenance of the body was the maintenance of the quest. The body and the quest were interdependent. The pact had to be preserved until the death of Hardrad, or evil would triumph again. Though the body could be harmed by no weapon, and his spirit was his weakness, the body could still be undone in the lapse when the body was without soul. All his efforts, all his strength, had to be invested in his inner character. The wounds of his soul had to strengthen it, to build his character into another bastion against evil. Now, he understood the true place that had to be reinforced. The place of vulnerability was inside him, and this was where his defences had to be built up. He could not depend on his allies to maintain the fortifications of his astral being, lest they tire and abandon the quest. He could not allow demoniac spectres to rob him of purpose and lead him astray again. There would be more challenges. More tests. He had to prepare. He had to restore the sacrificial coalition, reaffirm his strength and devotion, and rise as the leading participant. Direct control of the body was his alone. That made him the ruler of this pact of three.

'I am not like the Sephric lords,' Guidonis told him, 'there are many evils in this world, because there are many nations and people who seek slaves. Those who are good seek friends. They do not seek slaves or pawns. With my powers, I could have conquered slaves with ease. Yet, instead, I sought out friends. I made a coalition with you, rather than an empire. This proves that my purpose is good. Have faith in me, so that we may prevail. We will retain our commitment to goodness within, and we will still be able to bargain for redemption in the afterlife if we should die, because our designs were good during our time in the world. The reward of redemption may still greet us, with the accomplishment of the quest, if you achieve discipline and purpose. Our practices may have been similar to the ways of Hydra, but chose them only because they were strong. It does not affect the rightfulness of our designs.'

'I give you every commitment,' Michael declared, 'I swear that I will never allow fear and doubt to interrupt the course of this righteous quest again.'

And, with those words, Michael woke to find his body bound in shadow yet again. But this time, he was entangled quite thickly in sticky threads of spider silk, and no light could reach his hidden eyes. Very quickly, he understood the nature of his new prison. He was hanging from his feet, because the blood had rushed to his head and it was trying to force him back into unconsciousness. He had also been weakened and placed in a hallucinatory death-sleep by the venom that permeated his veins, but his unnatural resilience had protected him. During its unconsciousness, the body had become the property of the great spider responsible for the massive sticky web, which was one of many dark terrors inhabiting the shadow of the Grave Expanse.

Michael now believed Guidonis had been foolish to abandon the body in this lapse, despite the importance of his discovery of Kraide's spectral presence within his visions. Why had he, if he was so wise, not predicted the danger of abandoning the body in a region whose mere mention strikes terror into those who know the chronicles? But it soon occurred to Michael that he might have been equally responsible for his body's lapse in consciousness, through his decreased will to carry this body on as a weapon to accomplish the quest. He vowed not to allow feelings of doubt to reclaim the precious body, lest he experience a lapse like this again. His own soul's weakness should not be allowed to become an obstacle to the destiny of his country and the life and liberty of the innocents within. If he let go, and lost his determination, he would return to a state of darkness and adversity that would surpass any imaginable level of physical pain. His resilience would overcome the spider venom, and his determination would prevent his blood's pressure on his temples forcing him back into unconsciousness. The spider, wherever it lay, was just another wretched creature that would be exterminated for its error, if it dared to return before he escaped. He did not fear it, for he only suspected that it might delay him in carrying out his mandate.

Regardless of his imprisonment in the spider's silk, he was able to shift the position of his blade and lift it out of the sheath, so that it could be nudged to cut a strand of the silk. After this was accomplished, he was able to progressively slide the blade back and forth, until it slit the passage of his escape. Standing in the darkness, he knew that his body had strayed from the road during its unconsciousness, and he knew that it would be necessary to find some way back to the Highway, or he would be required to ascend the Forbidden Mountains by some other road.

Through many sinister trees, Michael walked, and the branches were of such grotesque forms that his eyes created countless illusions of ancient bones and skulls, staring malevolently at him from the black hollows of their eyes, entangled and forgotten there. In his attempt to depart from the spider's dining place, there was some swift movement among the shadows of the trees, but he did not discern its source. A rustling sound, perhaps made by the rush of many delicate limbs, became louder. It disturbed the dry forest floor below. The great spiders responsible for his prior captivity were not objects of fear for Michael, because he knew that far worse things existed in the universe, and the threat of some petty injury of the flesh meant little to him now. But they did possess the ability to slow his mission with their venom, and he would not tolerate that. As he proceeded onward, the moonlight crept in through the tall treetops and he saw the mother spider descending towards him, her frontal limbs outstretched in hope of snatching Michael and returning him to her nest.

The spider projected her frontal limbs onto the wanderer at his shoulders, and he turned in disgust. He cut back at them furiously with his sword, but his steel was not sufficiently strong to cut through the armour of her coarse projections. So he was forced to display his valour once more in combat with the beast. It is quite likely that cutting through between the segments of her limb would have been a sufficient punishment, but his mind was thrust back to his combat with Kraide in the battlefield of the

Three Stairs. The quest now commanded Michael only to slay the wicked lord Hardrad in Hydra's dark fortress, and to destroy his realm utterly. But all creatures obstructing his path were certainly meant to be slain also.

And the spider's legs were like the many heads of the serpent creatures the Sephric frames were as hosts to. The spider was not a mother of acceptable and natural creatures. This spider was an abomination, present only to slow Michael's quest, and it demonstrated this through its sheer aggression in their battle. Each of its limbs became weapons, as it repeatedly sought to impale and lift Michael to its venomous pincers. But Michael slashed through the joints between each limb, until he had finally cut each of the limbs from the beast. The creature remained alive but immobile, and rested in the pool of its misery, but Michael could not tolerate the continuation of its life, for his mission commanded him to slay it for coming between him and Hardrad's gates. So he stabbed through the multiple eyed head of the beast and cut through the mass of its back until the disgusting contents were spilled and it became cold and lifeless. So with the spider destroyed, he walked through the spilled slime of the monster and continued his quest, hoping that nothing else would be foolish enough to interrupt his journey and force him to subject it to the same gruesome act of slaughter.

Through the enclosures of the neverending forest, Michael continued in search of the way out. But even after slaying the smother spider of the forest, the rest of his journey was not tranquil, for as he continued to venture through the mass of tangled trees, he saw the movement of some swift and tall creature nearby. Now, the moon caught the eyes of many felines assembling before him in the shadows. But the creatures were not poised low down in the undergrowth as they scrutinised the traveller, for they were instead standing taller than Michael's own frame, and their stare was not in conformity with the expectations one has of wild animals. Rather their stare was more otherworldly, for it was akin to the glow of supernatural awareness in the eyes of the lords of Hydra themselves.

As he approached them fearlessly, they all shrieked deafeningly and descended on Michael, mauling him with claws like daggers and biting at him with razor sharp teeth. Swinging his sword like a scythe, he moved through the legion of slashing black figures and cut through each of them at the waist. They had tall and lean with bodies, very strong, like apes, but their heads resembled those of wild cats and the ears crowning these wild visages were stiff and tall projections like the horns of a gazelle or the ears of an attentive rabbit. Their agility was terrifying.

In his prolonged combat with the cat men in the forest, which took him until daybreak, Michael came to believe that they were the source of the many fearful tales the Rose had always had of the Grave Expanse. They were a pack capable of assailing any army of men in the night. And the reason they had not attacked the armies of Hydra was not a mystery. They were not worldly beings but demons made flesh, as the Sephric lords were. They disgusted Michael, and he felt compelled to annihilate the cursed creatures to the last one and hurl them back into the chasm of the Undergrave, but they fled with the coming of the sun through the skeletal treetops. He slew more than a hundred of them in the forest without fatigue, and his black attire took neither stain nor tear in the battle, for it was also under the protection of the quest's spectral guarantors.

Michael walked on, cleaning his sword and concealing it in his unstained robes again. He was a hooded and cloaked figure in commemoration of the image of Guidonis in life, and he was now completely devoted in unquestioningly loyal service to the monk's immortal spectre. The heretic was his guide, the key to his vengeance against Hardrad.

V. THE HARVESTER

The valley that led Michael to the towers of Hydran sorcery was like a prison of dark stone, because it was steep and bare on either side, and so sinister of design as to be sufficient evidence of the evil supernatural influences there. Even the fluctuations of the winds seemed to whisper foreboding curses through the labyrinth, which was surely a haven of unending malice. The towering formations of rock were twisted and chaotic in form, and many were made of blocks stacked in such a way that only unnameable powers could maintain them in that arrangement. There would frequently be a pattering sound, or a chorus of muttering, as if from a host of lost spirits that had long inhabited the place. Invisible hands seemed to be pushing the rocks and making them shudder. Although they rumbled, and small pieces would fall, no boulder came crashing towards the ragged figure of Michael, who, in his newfound determination, continued his travels in the guise of a hooded wanderer, and never looked back.

It became apparent to Michael that the place was severely infested by some dangerous breed of wild dog, because, several times, he glimpsed one cross his path, swift as lightning, and disappear down some shadowy avenue in the labyrinth. They did not make him fear the place, and the rocks that shook with their tremendous power, above, also failed to deter him. Nothing emerged to stop him, and Michael knew that none would dare, because all those entities that feed upon fear would find none of that food if they tried to look for it in him. He found a darker and more aggressive sky above him, as he proceeded to the nest of sorcery where he knew his enemy was hatching evil. Several bright crimson flashes came forth from the dark depths of the clouds, as if warning him to turn back. But he did not waver. The consequential mighty crashes of thunder made the rocks tremble in such a way that could only demonstrate their sentience. Yet Michael cared not for the mysteries of the place, because he had committed everything to the achievement of his mission.

As he marched on, knowing that he alone was stronger than any army walking the earth, his path led him through a small number of dead trees, and into an enclosure that offered no path forward, and he knew that something in Guidonis's wisdom had faulted. His path was blocked by a great stone boundary. When he became confused and was imminently to turn back, in his suspicions that a demon was leading him astray, having clawed and clawed until it found a weakness in Guidonis's powers, at last, he realised that the heretic had just conjured himself from the dust and was standing beside him. But Guidonis was not concerned about the demon of

Michael's suspicions, for there was no such entity, and the monk was looking above, to a precipice of dark stone, where a distant robed and crowned figure was leaning on a walking stick, observing *both* of them. The wizard looking down at them could see his ally, Guidonis, invisible though he was to the eyes of mortals. Michael knew that only a wizard of truly terrible power could perceive that there was another being accompanying him, for this meant that the Hydran sorcerer could detect his allies, even though they only existed as spirits, ever bathing him in supernatural power.

A voice, containing a terrible malicious intelligence and strange hypnotic powers, spoke like the thunder, 'I'm impressed. Like any soldier, bottling up your weaknesses and hiding behind this foolish student Guidonis, who knows nothing of the forces he seeks to manipulate. And your sister, a common wench who will be nothing but an impediment in your journey. It perplexes me that you chose her, of all the possible people who would have sufficed, to fill that void in your pitiful sacrificial alliance. But the three of you are going to be educated. Let this be a particular lesson to you, the heretical monk, who is but a pathetic student of these arts. You have told this soldier that he knows nothing and should follow your commands, as you have told the spirit of the slain whore from a destroyed Rose village. This is a lie. You know as little as they do, and you are well aware of this weakness, adventurer. You may be blinded by your crusading zeal, but they need not be. You will now learn the futility of your quest. Allow me to introduce you to the unfortunate by-product of your fatal experiment, risen from the shadows as you did, the slave that will erase your souls, consume this body and serve as our weapon, thereafter, to destroy Rose once and for all. Behold the forbidden entity, the Harvester, which your heretical ritual released it from its prison! It is your own soul's vacuum, a mouth more terrible than any beast in the mortal world, returned to take you into the Abyss where you belong!'

And the rock exploded all around them, creating dust to blind them, and the beginning of the catastrophic collapse of the mountain's stone, such that they could no longer see the wizard who had informed them of their impending doom. An unseen force, as transparent as the air but as strong as a dragon's tail, collided with them and cast them out of the stone enclosure so that they tumbled into the same dead trees they had passed through earlier. As they freed their robes from the branches, the evil force came following them, ploughing through the solid rock, like it was but sand. It crushed the dried trees like straw as it pursued them, but Guidonis remained, stood his ground and told Michael to flee. 'Go! Get the body out of here!' he commanded, 'I will find my way back to you!' And Michael was not hesitant to follow Guidonis's order, because he knew that the monk's superior knowledge of good and evil was the reason for his survival thus far. This was a science beyond his understanding, and he fled from the scene in childlike confusion. How a spirit could battle, as if it had physical form, was impossible for Michael to understand, at this stage in his journey, as such a being is already disembodied, and can hardly be slain. But this new enigmatic foe, against whom Guidonis battled, was hardly a mortal creature, for it was as much invisible to mortal eyes, and as much a ghost, as the heretic himself.

Guidonis applied an incantation that allowed him to perceive the form of his opponent, by letting himself fall into an astral space, outside of temporal existence, but intersecting it, where disembodied spirits can take refuge, which is called the Dark Plane. In that strange realm, there are many keys to the Undergrave, and sorcerers have oft used the Dark Plane to unlock occult knowledge. Within the plane, the sight can best be described as if one was constantly at the centre of a glass sphere, out in the dark among the stars, as though the stars were being projected around one, and moving about so quickly that it would make even the most disciplined sorcerer feel nauseous. The stars rushed back and forth, and disappeared, and new ones took their place, and many curious objects came into view above the monk. Within the Dark Plane, Guidonis was much stronger in battle with his foe, for he could catch the astral light of the stars fluctuating in the sky, and turn it into a mighty bolt of lightning that he could direct against the hulking entity. As magnificent as it seemed, directed lightning did little to deter the creature, and it continued to roar and stomp in his direction, until it stood like a black void against the sky, towering above the heretic. As the creature bellowed and charged at him, Guidonis leaped to escape its path, as if he were engaged in a bull-fight, and he used his magical hands to project a pale beam that seemed to enchain objects, and allowed him to drag rocks down from the sky. They crashed down upon the shadow being, but it only learned, and copied his example, growing long tentacles, sending them out towards the stars and grasping the peculiar objects offered in the farthest places of the universe. So the monster accumulated several cylinders of shining gold, and these objects appeared to be ornately decorated with the carved images of beings too otherworldly to envision, and violently hurled these peculiar vessels against the monk.

When the golden vessels fell beside him, by some science unknown, they created bizarre orange rays of heat that burned the stone by his feet as he ran to keep himself from the shadow creature's reach. But these peculiar forms of attack were not the work of Michael's deathly Harvester, because they were also directed against that creature until they gained its attention, and only succeeded in sending it into a terrible rage against them. The forbidden Harvester then went forward and crushed them into pulverised disks, strips of metallic material, and fragmented components glowing, that are too otherworldly to describe. As this happened, some strange laws of their alien science demanded their detonation, which lit the whole place up and blinded both of the duelling ghosts, until Guidonis recovered his sight, and the Harvester was no longer invisible. Some reaction, prompted by the energy released by the golden vessels, had caused the true form of their shadowy target to be exposed, and the very disturbing form of the hitherto invisible monster was revealed to Guidonis's sight in the process.

The Harvester, which was Michael's forbidden death guardian, unique to him, appointed to drag him to the afterlife, manifested before the heretic in the Dark Plane, and it looked like a hunchbacked giant, with a twisted neck and dislocated jaw. It had a bony and translucent body, emitting a terrible white glow, and everything about it resembled an oversized mutilated corpse being wielded by a demon. Its eyes were tightly shut, it eternally roared and drooled slime and blood onto the stone floor of the Dark Plane, and it moved without any indication of sensory awareness. It was only metaphysically aware, sensing souls and the means to devour them. The transparent tentacles that had previously shot from its body to take the golden vessels from the sky were acting autonomously, as if some other intelligence guided those appendages. It was not cognisant of the rock of the earth or of physical vulnerabilities, and it even ignored the foundations and elevations of stone that were protruding into the Dark Plane from the temporal realm. Knowing this, Guidonis devised the best way to slow this titanic embodiment of inner evil, which was the only option available, since it could never be destroyed.

His gambit would be a carefully timed incantation, to liquefy the rock of the mountain and dash through it, to trap the creature within the stone, although he knew that it would eventually find its way out of that trap and pursue the body again. He backed towards the mountains, which were still present in the Dark Plane, for they looked like great black shards standing against the cosmic wonders burning brilliantly in the sky. As he led the way, the relentless monster lumbered forward in pursuit. As he spoke the beginning words of the incantation, the creature threw lightning after him, and he was weakened. He had not known that it possessed this ability. It may have actually gained this ability in the wake of *his* foolish application of it earlier. As he slowed, one of its tentacles reached out and wrapped around his foot, and threw him against the rock. Having claimed the first component for the completion of its own quest, it proceeded to drag him away from his destination. It was dragging him back, away from the mountains! It was taking him to the body! Only if they were all taken and eaten together, *all three* in the sacrificial coalition, could it devour their souls and consume their power to strengthen its own evil.

Guidonis could not permit the creature to take him near the body of Michael, lest it eat them together and fulfil its purpose. That would make the whole quest, and the ritual that preceded it, seem like folly! He clawed the earth and the stone to slow his passage as he was dragged away. He knew that the body was near, and the monster could not be permitted to reach it. 'Michael! Stay away!' he warned, as he was dragged, 'do not let it take the body!'

Michael was certainly still fleeing the creature, which shattered barriers of stone in its pursuit of him, and it destabilised the foundations of one of the tall black mountains. His escaped shadow creature remained invisible to him, and Guidonis's spirit was also invisible because he was occupying its realm, but Michael knew the entity was present when it stamped the dead vegetation and shattered the columns and boulders that stood in its way. As the mountain broke asunder, and ended in a thunderous collapse of black boulders, the greatest chunk came between Michael and his demon, and blocked the narrow path of the creature as he fled. Seeing this opportunity, Guidonis spoke his incantation and the exposure of rock to his right fluxed and became passable to those in the Dark Plane, tempting the creature to move through it to find a path around the chunk that had blocked its path.

Now, Guidonis directed his curse so that the fluxed rock led the creature on a path deep into the foundation of the mountain, as it dragged him, until he was in a hollow deep inside the mountain. Here, he decided it would be a suitable prison to leave the demon, so he deactivated the curse and it stormed around, dragging him, but it dropped him down a chasm, and he landed in the shadow. There is always a means of sight in the Dark Plane, because beings glow there, but this chasm bore a deeper kind of shadow that Guidonis understood to be the signpost of a place where the boundary with the Undergrave is weak. In the making of the universe, there had surely been little need to seal off such little holes to the outer darkness of the cosmos, if they are in the deep places of the world, so the Constructor had ignored them. It had not been mankind's place to use sorcery to find these holes in the world, but, in their sin and their mischievous dispositions, they had done this, and unleashed greater evil into the world to plague them. It had been their curiosity, their irresponsible need to look at all things scientifically, and toy with their construction, that had birthed and unleashed all of the evil in the world.

To escape the engulfing dark, Guidonis crept from the shadows, and reached out with his magical hand, creating a new sphere of flux, to enable himself move through the rock like sand, and escape the mountain. But the sphere was closed by an arc of lightning from the hand of the Hydran magician, who had arrived by the same sorcery as he. 'You will not escape, unless you put yourself in our service!' the magician said, 'now it's time for your lesson! You will condition the body to serve us! Do not presume to use our own practices against us. The dark path is ours, and ours alone!'

But the Sephric magician soon learned that he was unwise to be there, because the lightning of Guidonis closed his escape aperture, where he fluxed the stone to create his own exit from the prison, and Guidonis's own lightning closed it as he did this. 'You underestimate me, Sephric,' he warned, 'go back to your lair. Soon you will go into never-ending destruction, and your king will follow.'

'You insolent student! Now I will just have to destroy you here!'

'You can't harm me. I'm not of this world, flesh-bag!' Guidonis shouted, 'your corporeality, your cowardice and your inability to endure pain will be your undoing.'

By speaking an incantation, the enemy sorcerer attempted to influence the forbidden Harvester and draw it to Guidonis, but he countered the curse with his own greater utterances. 'I have studied everything about you, Nefarion! Did you not think I became more powerful than you, before I embarked on this quest? None of your tricks will work on me!'

'You only delay the inevitable! The forbidden is unleashed. Your Harvester will hunt you to the edge of the world.'

'Then I shall need to kill you all the quicker!' the heretic monk answered, forming a sphere of burning heat over his palm, and hurling it, so that it pursued the Sephric. Because Nefarion was distracted by the approaching flames, Guidonis reopened the flux in the rock and entered it, but a tentacle shot onto his ankle from the rotten body of the Harvester, and the monster tried to follow, so he came back into the hollow and closed the exit. He would leave alone, and the Harvester would remain inside the mountain. It would be folly for Nefarion to attempt to release it from its prison, for it would likely kill him in the process. Now, part of the rotten tendril was trapped in the rock, because the stone had solidified according to the will of Guidonis, and the creature found this greatly painful. If Guidonis left the entity like this, it would be an even better form of imprisonment for it, because it would limit its mobility in the hollow, and it could not follow him if he sought to exit by another side of the hollow.

The dark wizard Nefarion dispatched a fireball, in a vain bid to vaporise the tentacle and free the entity, but Guidonis projected a shield of ice and blocked this, telling the dark sorcerer that he must leave the hollow and not return. Knowing that he could not maximise his powers in the darkness of this hollow, and it would be too dangerous to attempt to destroy the prison of the Harvester, Nefarion fled through a passage of fluxed rock and disappeared. To ensure that the sorcerer could not find the shadow creature and set it free in his absence, Guidonis put up several barriers of fire and ice around the entity, which would take many days to wane, and no counter-curses could speed the process. But he suspected that the Sephric would not return, for fear that his fortunes would be worse if he took part in a second duel in the hollow. Knowing that the prison would delay the deadly Harvester, though he could not be certain of the duration, the heretic monk made the stone yield again, and vanished away through the passage, seeking to be reunited with the lasting body that his quest depended upon.

When Guidonis emerged from the rock of the mountain, he exited from the Dark Plane, and saw the dark sky again, in its true form, a brewing black and scarlet storm of terrible power, circling the most imposing of the shadowy peaks. He found Michael there, waiting for him, with his sister. Why he had stopped and sought counsel from *her* at this time, the monk did not know, but it angered him. It angered him far worse, when the gleaming spirit of the martyr presumed to educate him, saying, 'you cannot conceal it forever, this quest is based upon a heretical act. Its consequences cannot be escaped by these temporary precautions.'

She was right. But he was not prepared to allow her to lecture him in the very science that he had pioneered. 'Are you the body's ruler?' he asked, in a mocking voice, 'the heresy is his, and he is engaged in it willingly. He selected the option of sacrifice, even of sacrifice leading to his eternal destruction. You, girl, have already been a sacrifice, sufficient enough to aid us. We need only your soul's presence. It was a ritual necessity. We do not require your counsel. The Constructor is merciful, and will probably not allow your involvement in this quest to damn you. But I see a darker fate awaiting Michael, and he goes willingly into it. It is the only way. Doom himself, or doom humanity? It's obvious what is best.'

'The Constructor of all things chastises whom he will,' she responded, but mighty and furious thuds against stone subsequently came, from within the mountain, and they knew that the hulking embodiment of their doom was attempting to escape, driven unendingly by its own quest to collect the body of Michael and release their three souls to the next life.

'You delay us!' Guidonis said to silence the girl, and he bade Michael to continue the quest under his guidance alone. When Michael was infused with the knowledge of Guidonis again, he understood that his opponent in the hollow of the mountain was Nefarion, the infamous Sephric teacher of all Hydran magic. His existence had been known, but few among the Rose people dared to speak his name. That he had referred to the "heretical" nature of Guidonis's power, to condemn his ways, seemed absurd, for Nefarion himself had surely committed such heresies tenfold already. But the heresy of Nefarion had been perfected as an art of evil, because he was the heir to the long line of Sephric sorcerers, which dated back to the founding of their terrible house. And Nefarion's purpose, like all the Sephrics, was evil, and so his methods reflected his designs, whilst the three souls guiding the body of Michael knew of an ultimately good conclusion that they were seeking. The quest's end would be good, and the methods used to accomplish it were acceptable, as long as they succeeded.

VI. HAND OF THE COVEN

When he reached his destination, Michael found two growling Hydran watchmen in their black garb and armour, guarding the doorway into the dark Tower of Storms, which was the abode of Nefarion. They crossed their weapons to prevent the passage of the hooded traveller, and said something in their foul speech. By their tone, Michael assumed that they commanded him to stop. He drew his sword from his robes and held it high before them, telling them to depart this evil place to avoid its impending righteous annihilation, and escape the death that would be dealt to anyone courageous or foolish enough to stand between him and his Sephric target. And, although they did not understand his foreign words, they understood his meaning, because of the magic exerted by his increasingly strong mind upon them. In spite of his great power, their minds were like loyal dogs under the master of the tower, and they responded with mockery, as if he was none other than a foolish wandering monk, who had brandished a sword without any knowledge of how it was to be wielded.

They turned their weapons at him, to skewer him, and he responded by lunging close between the pikes, so that their length made them useless, grasping the weapons in his hands and pushing them away, before delivering fatal strikes through the shoulders of the two men with his own blade, and left their fallen bodies to empty their life's blood on the doorstep of Nefarion's lair. They had behaved like demons, and the hatred contained in their eyes had been the same as the Sephric malice, so they were surely puppets, and their lives were worthless. He proceeded into the ancient black fortress's hallway, and was surprised that there was neither guard, nor demon, nor magician inhabiting the place. But the mists of deception were in the air, and Michael knew better than to trust what he could see. Something was hunting him.

'Guidonis, where are you? I require your wisdom. Tell me what creature hunts us.'

'You will find that this place is truly empty, just as it appears, so you can trust your body's mortal senses,' the heretic replied, and Michael's eyes detected him emerge from the shadows, as if he had somehow been inside the stone of the tower's walls. But, when Michael stepped forward with his guide at his side, the latter froze, and he was wise to do the same.

'Wait!' Guidonis commanded, and he seemed to breathe deeply, as if he could read the presence of some camouflaged malice in the dryness of the air throughout the hallway. For several minutes, he closed his eyes and bore a look of intense concentration, warning Michael to remain silent. 'A coven was bound here.'

A feeling of severe dread chilled the blood in Michael's veins. He was still not yet invincible. He was bound by sorcery. And, by sorcery, he might yet be undone. But what could happen? His flesh would heal if balls of flame were cast at him, for he had experienced worse wounds before. His body would break out of any kind of prison, because it was not bound by such temporal limitations. No prison of sorcery could contain him in the manner that the embodiment of his soul's grief and terror, known as his Harvester, had been locked in the mountain. But what of a coven of magicians? Such a coven might seek to act as a living prison, maintained by the constant power of the hands of witches, to slow him indefinitely, and prevent his quest's end. He was not certain of this, because he knew little of this science, but he believed that Guidonis shared his fears.

Guidonis gestured for Michael to move forward, toward the doors that would lead deeper into the tower, but the monk did not speak. Michael knew that Guidonis was not temporally present, like he, and no mortal man on earth would have been capable of hearing the heretic's words if he spoke, but this monk's spirit chose to remain silent, and this seemed strange to Michael. But Guidonis was wise to be silent, because his astral presence could still be read, or the whispers of his spirit heard, by anyone attuned to the same arts as he. So the ghost of the monk went forward with Michael, the two of them moving like a pair of terrifying spectres inhabiting the black tattered robes, driven by sleepless wisdom and anger, but only one of them carried a sword and was visible to mortal eyes.

Carefully, Michael pushed open the doors and saw inside a chamber beyond the dark stone hall. There, under the light of the lamps that burned on the ceiling, he encountered the cold and deadly eyes of a grotesque Hydran witch, the first female of the enemy realm he had yet encountered, for he had only ever slain their men on the battlefield. She was accompanied by several others, but Michael did not count how many, for he had little time to act. Still holding his sword high, with strength enough to deal death with one strike, he bore no compassion for these witches, and he would not have wanted to let them escape, even if they had fallen to their knees and forsook their wicked nation. He intended to kill them, as he would any soldier, and hope that it surprised the Hydrans that their enemies were capable of the same brutality as they. But his hand was delayed, either by his confusion at the sight of such a bizarre coven of foes, or by some spell they put on hum. It was a delay enough to let them speak an incantation, and he heard Guidonis tut, in disappointment, as if the whole matter was trivial. He was thrown back into the hall, and pinned against the pillar by some terrible force like a great wind. As the sorceresses approached, through the doors, Guidonis stood beside them, invisible to their sight, and did not intervene, instead merely watching the thwarted assassin expectantly.

Although his hands were being pushed back against the stone of the pillar with great force, as the Hydran witches approached him, he succeeded in putting his left hand forward and felt the heat in his fingertips as he manifested fire above his palm. When it was too hot for him to hold any longer, he released it to one of the sorceresses, whose pale face was consumed in flame so that a charred mass replaced it, and she fell to her resting place on the cold floor. But Michael only cried out in pain, because his hand was now skeletal too, reduced to a horribly scarred form in the wake of its first attempt to wield the magical flames. Had he been mortal, and attempting to learn magic, this gambit would surely have killed him instantly. The witches were incapable of fear because they all acted as one, so they ignored their fallen sister, bringing rope, and they proceeded to bind their captive to the pillar as he groaned in agony. But his charred hand rapidly reconstructed itself. By the powers of Guidonis and Berenice, it put up new sinews, muscles and veins against the bone. The most crooked aged of the magicians was surprised and expressed something in the Hydran tongue with intrigue in her voice, for the Sephrics certainly knew none of the secrets of such power, and the one who wielded such powers could surely be seeking only the destruction of that house.

Knowing that Michael was impervious to all weapons mortal and immortal, the witches were ready to make their methods more sinister than the intruder's mere execution. So they looked at their cloaked captive in silence, for a moment, before all of them but their leader uttered a Hydran expression with one strong voice, acknowledging the plan that her telepathic mind had already given to them. In a single terrible voice that became an intense chorus of croaking, they spoke an incantation. The incantation came like thunder, and its effects upon Michael's flesh were as harsh and as sudden as lightning. He felt painful crystalline growths within his flesh, and he became a statue of stone. As his vision faded, he saw the face of Guidonis looking over him, shaking his head in dissatisfaction, and the image became a blur.

Then, Michael strayed out of the world and was in the Dark Plane, trapped among the veils that separate the rock of the Earth and the shadow of Hades. When he was there, the twelve witches were there with him, but they were no longer simply defined by their basic appearance of hideous agedness like before. Their flesh now appeared to be excessively scarred, weathered, corrupted and burned, and they were far more unsightly. A sinister light shone from their eyes, and it was very piercing, staring through Michael's stone body, with greater power and knowledge than he had seen in the Sephric General Kraide. There had been thirteen, but one of the women was lying slain by his hand's fire. The whole of the fallen witch's body appeared as bones on the floor in the Dark Plane, despite the fact that only her head had been taken by the flames in Michael's observation of her death in the temporal plane.

The twelve women only stared at him as he remained in his prison of stone, and Michael believed that they intended to keep him here until the Harvester, which had been successfully encased in the mountain by Guidonis before, escaped. It would seek him out, and smash the tower, to find him and the spirits that guided him, so that it could partake in the ritual eating of him and his ghost companions. By this method, his immortality could be undone. It was the only option, the only possible objective of Nefarion and his witch students, in their bid to destroy the assassin.

Now, some of the wretched common soldiers of Hardrad's realm rushed through the doorway of the hazy dark hall of pillars. They came from deeper in the tower, and they were carrying a great black cauldron with them. They placed the cauldron at the foot of the pillar that bound Michael in stone, and the pale witches reached out with withered hands and sharp claws to his own scorched hand, seeking to detach him from the column. But his hand was no longer scarred, and had become a fist of stone, so that it was much stronger, and would not yield. When the witches tried to take him down and lower him into the cauldron, he knew that he could not permit it, so he focused his mind on his body, and took control of the stone. It no longer served as a prison, but a newfound shield against them.

When he took up the stone body as his preferred form, Michael came out of the Dark Plane as easily as it is to pass from one chamber to another, so that the appearance of the place returned to an earthly reality, and he found that he controlled a hulking monstrosity of stone flesh as his body. He was capable of fearsome strength, and he threw the cauldron across the room in his determination, which splashed acid in the room, and the droplets stung when they struck him, and made holes like bores through the stone of his body. He knew, now, the terrible purpose of the cauldron and the transformation of his body into stone. The coven had sought to take his body and dissolve him in the acid. They would then suspend him in some solution to imprison him forever in Nefarion's Tower. Instead, the acid was thrown onto the witches, and it quickly completed the journey their hellish arts had set them on, for it reduced them to molten blood and bone as they cried out in torment and horror. Contained within their screams, there might perhaps have even been enough humanity to inspire pity and remorse, but the spirit of Guidonis purged this weakness, and the heart of Michael was as black as the robes that had cloaked him on his sleepless journey.

The aged leader of the witches, who possessed the sinister light of ancient wisdom and the knowledge of the power of the Sephric House in her wrinkled face and shrewd eyes, recoiled in fear and doubt, and Michael turned on her with his heart and hands of stone, crushing her into the stone, so that she shrieked hideously and only a pool of death remained. Like a siege engine, he smashed the foundations of the tower, so that it shook, but he was unable to bring the place tumbling down, because more than its foundations of stone kept it erect. Avoiding the expanding pool of spilled acid, he lumbered in pursuit of the fleeing Hydran witches and soldiers through the dark corridor beyond the doorway, which offered a way deeper into the tower's refuges. The place was lit by torches, but the magic of the witches dimmed them to deter his passage, and they were finally extinguished. Touching the stone as he went, Michael guided himself through the tower, and he found a junction.

Lighting the stone passage, he encountered a fair figure standing before him, and he took her for one of the unforgivable sorceresses creating an illusion of beauty for ways of deception, and raised his stone fist. But he looked into her fearless and wise eyes, which were like beacons of the same light that binds the universe, and there was something familiar within, so that he could not destroy her. Berenice, his sister. What brute would raise its hand against her image, and insult her perfect martyrdom? A martyress fallen once is a martyress immortal, and she would never fall again. As he lowered his hand in apology, he thought about her purpose in the quest, and he came to understand that she was his guiding light, just as Guidonis was his map. When darkness prevailed, her light would come and conquer the shadow, and Michael would have sight again. What Guidonis gave him in knowledge, she gave in illuminating judgment. He could not go anywhere without her counsel.

'You are made of stone?' she said to him, 'how were you put into this state?'

'The witches did this to me,' he answered.

'You are bound by enchantments that keep you as a structure of living matter. Not a cold statue. As soon as you were turned to stone, the enchantments ceased to have any effect on you.'

'It is the work of sorcery,' he croaked, 'I cannot change it.'

'This is the point in the quest where you will have to take up the authority to create your own counter-curses. Will you wish yourself to remain a statue of stone, because of the strength it has lent you?' she asked.

'Because of my stone structure, I have been able to demonstrate great strength, but it is not my wish remain a statue like this. In this state I am vulnerable to any manner of destruction as long as the enchantments of Guidonis cannot aid me.'

'But we are the makers of our fates, and you are being misled somehow. Just now, when you reached this junction, you might have attacked me, but I am already dead. If you wish it, then you will cease to be bound in this structure of stone. You will be restored. The body obeys your commands and so you are capable of any enchantment you wish to use. You need utter nothing. Just think it.'

133

He thought about her words, and some amount of warmth seemed to be returned to his heart and soul. His muscle and skin ceased to be stone, and he became human again, and looked down in shame because of his blind hostility to her, unable to meet her eyes. She was right. This form, as a strong being like a moving statue of stone, was being sustained only by his mind's own work. All sorcery is a duel, between mind and fate, for lordship over the body, for mind may avert even the most terrible fate, if it is strong enough. Through his sister's wisdom, his mind was strong, and she carried him out from of this shell of stone, and breathed pure life back into him, so that he could continue on his quest and destroy the master of Hydran sorcery.

But Guidonis soon materialised from the air and was standing between Michael's and his fair sister. And the robed heretic seemed foul, the way a bat-winged herald of woe would appear if it stood and eclipsed an angel of light. There was a discontented look in the shadowed face below the hood of the monk, but Guidonis did not speak. He only looked sullenly at the body, which was the crucial of the quest. He felt no pain for the quest, so this had to mean pain ulterior. He became angry with Michael's sister and told her not to interfere, hissing, 'now look what you did! You have robbed him of his greatest shield against the magicians, for they had no idea what they had created in their attempts to imprison the body as a stone.' As he said these words, his face was very close to Berenice's own, and it looked to Michael as though he was trying to sink his teeth into her neck, while staring directly into her eyes with fury. 'Your interference in the quest is becoming troublesome' he continued, 'you are proving to be more troublesome than useful to the body. You and I will discuss the matter of your intolerable impudence away from the body's ears. You must understand your function within this operation.'

'So is this body not still occupied by a soul of its own?' Berenice retorted, 'is his consent not required to maintain the body?'

When she said this, Guidonis regarded her harshly from his hood's shadow, and concluded the quarrel when he snapped, 'go back to your nest,' and she went away into the shadows, and seemed to be distressed, as though she had more to say, but was afraid to speak. This troubled Michael. He dared not risk summoning her back for counsel, lest Guidonis lose faith in him and punish him again, as he had done in the Grave Expanse. He would do nothing to jeopardise the body and the quest.

'She's a fool, of course!' the heretic scoffed in the martyress's absence, 'take no heed of her weakness. This girl is the source of all the

135

weakness in the quest. I should have predicted, in the beginning, that the involvement of a female intelligence would only undermine our quest. In time, her influence will diminish, a fading tide against the rock of our covenant, and she will be purged. But that is not yet possible. You must be strong, and be my student. You must adopt my philosophy, and have no mercy. You took fire into your hand for the first time at the pillar, but you did it without wisdom to stabilise it and control it. Nonetheless, this is a great step. In time, you will become as powerful as I. And, later, the body will make you even more powerful than I or any creature that walks this Earth.

'So let us go to the Hydran wizard Nefarion! Let us rob him of his life, his knowledge, and his instruments. Let us turn his own powers on him, as we continue our journey to undo the black-hearted realm of Hardrad, even if we must sneak into his accursed lair like a serpent in the night, and kill him by the most treacherous means! These Sephrics, who have fought against humanity without honour, are the only creatures whose wrongs are rightfully corrected by the most violent means, and they all deserve to be reduced to blood, bones and ash, in all haste. Fill your mind with the vision of the rotten Hydran king in his demise, who once presumed himself the master of the human race, but has been drowned in his own blood by your hand. Let the quest's end fill your mind. And go on to its accomplishment!'

So Michael, inspired by the promises of Guidonis, emptied his sister's voice from his mind, and went on with his guide, his heart as cold and hard as the stone that he had been liberated from. After he heard the words of Guidonis, his sister's involvement in the quest seemed absurd, because she was truly no more than a mere girl, present only because ritual necessity demanded a third spirit in the quest. She may have experienced martyrdom, and she may have earned a place close to the universe's Constructor, but many a fool is capable of these same accomplishments. He was ashamed of his infatuation with the spirit of Berenice. The ways of Guidonis told him that innocence is the first refuge of stupidity, and martyrdom is the ultimate path of those fools, obtaining death during their innocence, but that comes about only because they were too weak and foolish to raise a weapon. Though redemption in death is perhaps accessed by this doorway of gentleness, it is always certain to be accomplished with ease by the stupid, while the wise have better paths to take, for they have greater designs to fulfil. And knowledge and wisdom prevail over fear, for they know no bounds, and the hand can achieve any accomplishment by such guiding light, which provides all-piercing vision.

Guidonis praised Michael's use of enchanted fire-throwing, and this pleased him. He gained a great feeling of power and passionate devotion when he looked at the palm he had scorched with the fire. It was indeed an accomplishment, although he had believed it to be in error at the time. But, when he released the fire against one of his unholy captors in the hallway, he had been restrained by the power of the witches' incantation pushing him up against the pillar. In such a severe state, to manifest and dispatch a sphere of fire had surely been a feat! Now, he remembered the looks upon the faces of the witches as they fled. They knew nothing of the power they faced! This was the very power that Michael and Guidonis would bring against the Sephrics until their house was ended, and their realm was taken apart. Michael was the sword of Rose, the blade that had been made by secret ritual forgery, to pierce the black heart of Hydra.

With his hand healed, so that it was ready and strong, Michael carried his sword, and followed the lead of Guidonis, so that they ascended the stone funnel of the main tower, which had poisonous black and crimson fumes billowing up in search of escape at the summit. As he ascended the spiralling stair, he felt the fumes intensify, and looked down to the source as he ran, whereupon he discovered that the dark fluid was bubbling and rising in his pursuit. The perilous potion seemed to carry the bones and the dissolved wings of a bat in it, and produced an evil stench that was many times worse than that familiar odour of the rotting corpse, which had tormented Michael many times during the plight of Rose. But Guidonis instructed him not to linger and look upon the coming liquid, because even this body's immortal flesh could be hindered if it came into contact with the concoction. Such a delay would not be acceptable. With each passing moment, that terrible wraith of his subconscious darkness, his Harvester, was surely freeing itself from its stone prison in the roots of mountains, and it would set out in his pursuit again. When he remembered the blunt power of the shadow creature, the idea came upon him of using the creature's rock-splitting power like an invisible mace against the fortifications of Hydra, if he could attract the entity's fury against the walls. Such an option might throw down the Tower of Nefarion, should he remain here and wait for the creature's coming.

The boiling soup of his doom was ascending, and Michael and Guidonis were in flight up the spiralling stair, until they came to the top of the tower, where they rediscovered their target, the dark wizard. There was a shining black floor on the tower top, and it was adorned with the image of a white many-headed serpent, with the magical well in the centre, from whence the torrent of poisonous fume emerged and ascended into the tortured black sky. It generated the rotating storm, high above, and it shot red lightning down and empowered the hands of the magician of the tower. There was a great bat, possibly some demon in the service of Nefarion, circling in the shadow of the storm, mistaking the darkness for the cover of night, and Michael knew that this deception was counted among the many purposes of the Tower of Storms. His mind drew an immediate link between this winged monster and the ingredients that he had observed in the rising poison below. One of the constituents was surely a slain bat, much like the creature above. Perhaps the concoction was drawing the circling bat, and it would meet its doom there, because Nefarion required it to sustain the storm in all its shadow and its crimson energies.

Nefarion regarded them wrathfully, and the power of his words shook the foundations of the tower, when he said, 'I see both of you, but I also know there is another! I see a pitiful girl who perished among the other vermin that begat her! You are not cloaked behind this monstrosity that is your weapon! I bid all three of you to show yourselves, for I can destroy you all.'

'No! Remain concealed!' Guidonis commanded the girl's watching spirit, 'we must not all be weakened together! You must remain outside of the battle, so that you can heal the body if it is defeated!'

'The body! I only need the body to undo your covenant against Hydra!' Nefarion mocked, and his voice was much more terrible and almost subdued Michael when he commanded, 'surrender!'

But Guidonis was powerful, and he and Michael were sufficient to challenge the master of all Hydran sorcery. They all looked upon a lower mountain, which broke asunder as the trapped Harvester finally escaped its prison, and Guidonis told Nefarion that his tower would soon lie in ruin. So the Hydran magician wasted no more time boasting, to no avail, to persuade his foes into retreat, because he knew that the dark creature which sought to reap the three spirits of the body would fiercely assail the tower to find them, and all his property would fall into ruin if the tower toppled, and he would have failed his house. He resolved to use his hell-inspired voice to instruct the oppressive sky, and called down bolts of crimson light against his worst foe, who was Guidonis. He knew that it was futile to attack the body, so he made the monk his target. The lightning did seem to weaken the monk, who tried to shield himself with an unidentified projection of blue fire he manifested around him, but it was subdued by the crimson light, and he disappeared from Michael's sight.

Michael did not fear the sorcerer, and he knew that Guidonis would return, for he was already an incorporeal being, and even a sorcerer's weapons could do little to subdue such an entity, and could only harass it or drive it away into some prison for a time. As he fought the evil magician, Michael felt the healing powers of his dear sister repairing his flesh, and he knew that Guidonis was gone out of him, as if no longer bound to his body or quest. The monk's place in the quest had been weakened by Nefarion's lightning, as though only two remained. If Nefarion displaced the other healer, Berenice, his body would be vulnerable to all the powers of the sorcerer. Then, he would be undone. But it would not come to that. Berenice was present only as a healing influence, so Nefarion was incapable of directly affecting her with any power he could summon.

As he fought, Michael mustered every skill in his possession, and cast fire at the sorcerer many times, but the sorcerer took the fire into his robes and somehow kept it burning there, without spreading, and Michael knew that the magician's knowledge of this science was certainly far beyond his own. At last, Nefarion directed his sleeves at Michael, and released the concealed flames in a torrent, like a river of torment pouring directly at the assassin. As he stepped aside, to avoid the torrent of flame, the struggling assassin nearly stumbled off the tower's edge. He looked down towards the foot of the tower, and the whole fortress of Nefarion shook as some titanic entity came upon it, and thundered. It was scaling the tower, to fulfil its mission to harvest three spirits at the top, but it could not do it. The Harvester was heavy, like a statue of stone cast in its size, and it was also as wide as a great keep, but the tower was thin, so the Harvester would surely collapse it when it reached half the height of the tower.

Michael saw the shadowy shape of the creature at the foot of the tower, because Nefarion's storm illuminated the place with a light as unnatural as the Harvester, and the monster was a strong and broad black titan, its head crowned with two long, pointed shapes, like swords upon its head, but whether they were more akin to a rabbit's ears or a gazelle's horns was not evident to Michael, for he did not like to look at it. Its form terrified Michael more than Nefarion's own magic, for it was shaped in the form of his own darkest visions, and his nightmares had crafted it specifically to appeal to the heights of his own guilt and terror. In childhood, he once had a black rabbit as a pet, and it was dear to him, and he had been haunted by its death and strange visions of its ghost, which were probably induced by otherworldly devils, for Hydra had unleashed many strange horrors into the land of Rose. Now, he believed it was returning to him, a companion of his Harvester ascending the tower. He had no intention to be reunited with it. He had to escape that monster, at any cost. But it would never stop, until it found him and fulfilled its horrible purpose. All of his thoughts were on the

Harvester, not on Nefarion, even as the Hydran sorcerer dragged him, in his confusion, and cast him down into the bath of poison.

He fell into the poison, but was numb, so that he could not feel the pain, because his senses were all dead. His soul was gripped with terror, for it knew of the approaching dark. This position, deeper into the well of the tower, was near the Harvester. The Harvester was coming. He could hear its crashing limbs as it scaled the tower in search of the top. 'Guidonis!' He gasped from the concoction, 'Guidonis! Please! Offer me your wisdom! Berenice! Your light! Offer me hope! I cannot do this alone!'

The poison rose up, and it carried Michael to the top of the well from whence he had been thrown, where he could see Nefarion looking down in search of him through the liquid, with triumph in the glow of his Sephric eyes, even though his tower's destruction at the hands of the Harvester was imminent. Only the need to escape the Harvester was driving Michael to liberate himself. The Hydran magician had to perish, not because Michael's quest necessitated this deed, but because Nefarion was now in the way. He had to get away, to escape! So Michael put his blistered hand out, and dragged the shocked wizard Nefarion down with him, with terrible force, into the poison. Only now, did Michael realise how resistant he had proven to the potion, for it quickly attacked and tortured the flesh of the sorcerer who had brewed it, and he writhed like a drowning insect in it. He shrieked in an inhuman manner, and changed. He contorted, and seemed to grow the face of a serpent, as his back hunched and wings like a bat's shot forth, as though he sought to assume the shape of a dragon. But Michael drove his sword through the creature's heart, and dragged his own numbed carcass from the liquid. So the tower was crowned with three victorious beings, one flesh and two astral; two of them men in dark robes, the other a lady in heavenly white garments.

The Tower of Storms shook and shattered, ending the power of Nefarion, as the three stumbled, and their Harvester ascended, tearing the tower down. Michael was still paralysed with terror and weakness, and knew not what to do, but Guidonis called to the great winged mount from above. The bat of the tower descended in search of a new master, and found a being equally terrible, the assassin, so it accepted him as its new rider. It dutifully offered itself as the mount of its new master, and Michael took up his place on its back, and rode away through the storm, in the dark of night, in flight from the Harvester, and in search of his next Sephric foe, in his quest to bring their house to ruin. The Harvester bellowed in frustration, for it would have to travel many miles, in pursuit of the assassin, into the lands of Hydra.

As he entered the Dark Realm, Guidonis provided Michael with visions that contained revelations about the nature of the Hydran enemy. As he meditated, and the bat continued to carry him through the night, Michael saw the ancient ancestor of the Sephric House, as a mere common boy, before he came under the influence of Hades. It was not he, but a young girl at play, nearby, who was first taken by a wandering serpent's eyes and they drew her to the creature, until she lifted it and let down her throat. It vanished into her mouth, and the malevolent serpentine light of the Sephrics came into her own eyes, because she became the queen of the realm of darkness that had begun to pervade the world. The serpent had taken up residence in a human body. She took the other serpent up in her hands, which sought its own host, and brought it to the lad. He was not as quick to embrace such mischief, but then he saw the glow that seemed so powerful, so wise and so fair in the eyes of the serpent, which the girl was offering up to him, and he knew that he had to possess it as his own. So the boy, who would later be fearfully known as the first Sephric Father, accepted his own terrible gift, and went about doing mischief, which foreshadowed the nightmarish centuries that would remember his line as the most terrible source of tyranny in the history of mankind. The girl would also be his accomplice, just as the queens of Hydra would forever be the accomplices of their kings, equal in their wickedness.

When they were sought out, and beaten in punishment for their evil, the boy and girl only laughed and mocked the mortals who sought in vain to punish them. So the villagers resolved instead to drive them out, and the two fled because they knew the risk of an inquisitor coming in the belief that they were witches. Their place, thereafter, was in exile among the mountains that accompany a terrible peak bearing a rumoured incision, a passage to the Undergrave.

They came of age at the foot of the Northern Volcano, where stone falls down into the fires of the abyss, and they lived as spouses in the valley of shadow, with many cursed children possessed by the same dragons inhabiting the bodies of all Sephrics. After many long years in the exploration of sorcery, the family mixed a strange poison into the water supplies of the nearby settlements, which turned the inhabitants into the mounts of demons. They became an army of slaves. Now, the villagers were nothing but the soulless hybrids of men and pernicious demons of death, ready to be the instruments of their dark king. So the king made his castle, at the same settlement where his body had first been stolen by the serpent, and his line birthed the descendants of the Sephric House, until they were the established ruling House over the Hydran nation.

VII. Fall of the Assassin

The bat served very well as a winged mount for Michael's journey, for it proved capable of incredible speeds, and so it bore the body through the night until the sun rose and the creature longed for refuge in the shadows, so Michael dismounted it on the frozen heights that he found in the heart of the land of Hydra. But he knew the faithful bat was aided by magic, and it would be listening for his call, and would gladly return in his hour of need, as long as that hour found him concealed by night or the shadow of black clouds. His heart rejoiced for his discovery of this unlikely ally, the bat, which had found redemption from the dark purposes of its creation, by learning to serve a mission of light. It was surely like any beast, and knew nothing of good and evil, so it could only believe Michael to be the successor of its previous rider, because he was sustained by the same art of black sorcery.

Now, as he stood high on these cold hills, he assessed his location and the direction towards his destination, and he knew, through the mind of Guidonis, that a great Sephric stronghold lay to the east, so he set off in search of it, without fear of what may be waiting for him there. As he made his way across the cold hills, he huddled tightly in his robes and kept his bald head under his hood, because the northerly winds were getting stronger, and made a howling sound through the many withered plants protruding from the snow.

By this time, Michael's pains in the quest had made him stern, and he had learned much of the realities of sorcery, so he was not quite prone to mistake the mundane sounds of the wind in the thickets for the wailing voices of ghosts, even in the heart of the dreaded realm of Hydra. He knew that many mortals would have made such errors, if they were in his stead, because of their fearfulness and their superstitious notions about these forsaken lands. Yet Michael did stop, for, later, a voice did cry out to him, and it haunted him because it seemed like fell words were being spoken by a wicked being who had foreseen his fate and wanted to speed him to his doom. Now, he looked into the white distance as he stood on the heights, and he thought that a shadow crept onto the land and took the form of a rabbit's head, and it was as an omen to him. This was a terrible warning that his own Harvester was projecting itself, attempting to reach him from afar. It was surely still hundreds of miles away from him, because he last saw it scaling Nefarion's tower at Hydra's southern limits in the mountains. It was a heavy creature, and could probably only lumber a little faster than a man running, but he anticipated that it could certainly reach his current location within only a few days, for nothing could oppose its passage across Hydra. He thought about this danger, and decided that the winged mount of Nefarion would again be his only means of escape, if the Harvester should find him. He was dependent on it, now. He had, in a way, truly become the *successor* of the dark wizard Nefarion.

Somewhere to the east, there was a notable column of smoke rising, certainly from a fortress. Michael did not heed the spectre that incessantly drifted around on the heights and tried to haunt him, for his determination to fulfil his quest was icier than the hills he trod. At last, the spectre came and manifested near Michael, on the heights, and it bore his father's face and voice. Although Michael did not summon him, the sullen spirit of Guidonis came and stood, in dark garments identical to his own, at his side as he confronted his father.

'Why are you doing this, Michael, my son?' his father asked.

'I am committed to the quest for you, and for many others, also,' he answered, 'nothing can stop me, now'.

'You accomplished all that was necessary, when the General was assailed at the Three Stairs. The army of Hydra was destroyed, and they would never return. Why do you seek to personally lay waste to this forsaken land, which is already destined to fall into ruin? Surely all you are seeking is personal satisfaction! Evil though the Hydrans may be, and especially evil their king, are you not drowned in your thirst to obtain some other sort of vengeance? I warn you not to become deaf to the stern voice of righteousness, which forbids heresy and witchcraft! Be free of this quest, and let your spirit rest, so that we can be reunited as we stride towards a better, higher form of liberation!'

'And go where?' Michael questioned, in a mocking voice, 'I can sustain myself forever! Why should I give it up? So the Constructor can provide forgiveness and eternal life, as our narrow religion promises? Eternal life! What do I need it for? I can obtain the same immortality from Guidonis, and still obtain my vengeance! I have discovered my destiny in this sorcery! You only fear our science, because you do not understand it. Our science has already thwarted your redundant Constructor many times. You only fear the Constructor because you are like a child, who has not grown enough to become disillusioned with the hitherto infallible promises of his father.'

'You are overconfident, Michael. This war is far from over. I fear great pain waits for you in the fortress of Draco, which you now approach. You must not take that path. If you go, you may be unable to perish like an ordinary body, but you will be damaged beyond repair. You will be changed in such a way that all the healing powers you have acquired will suddenly become useless.'

'You foolish old man!' Michael mocked, 'nothing can harm me! I have seen my capabilities. You cannot comprehend what powers have been invested in me. Now leave me to the quest!'

'Let me counsel my daughter!' Michael's father demanded, 'she is still an innocent. I do not want her to be covered in blood and filth forever, by committing to this dirty quest of destruction. Michael, I denounce you again, for your arrogance, just as I condemned you for your cowardice before. I see that you have fallen further into ruin than I or anyone who perished in the tragedy at Loom, and your survival was no blessing, but a curse. You have taken to witchcraft and dug a grave for yourself more terrible than we could even wish for Hardrad, our accursed enemy.'

Guidonis broke his cold silence and spoke for himself and his student alike, when he said to Michael's father, 'the foolish wench is still our necessary ally. She has no need to see you! She is a fool, and easily swayed to either side in this debate, and we cannot let the restless spirit of her father interfere, while she is still a good aid in the quest. It is still a ritual necessity to include her in the quest. We cannot allow you to interfere in these important matters!'

'Then I hope that she escapes you, and forsakes the monstrosity of this body, and wishes it to return to the dust, from which it was conjured up,'

Although Guidonis and Michael were deaf to her precise words, because they had no interest in hearing her, Berenice's voice did come through weakly on the wind, like a very young girl, and she seemed dazed, and said, 'father, release me!'

'Daughter!' her father cried out, in grief.

'Away with you!' Guidonis commanded, directing his bony hand at the spectre and uttering a curse that sent out a shockwave, driving the entity away, dazed and confused, so that it went away to mourn its son's horrible fate, and dwell in various miserable and confused thoughts as it wandered the cold heights. Berenice then remained concealed, and was still bound to the quest, trying not to think of her father, because she was immersed among the same dominant thoughts of two strong-willed spirits, and they were beginning to eclipse her in their power over the destiny of the body. They knew that they would decide the outcome of the quest. Berenice's helpfulness was rapidly diminishing.

Michael did not heed the warnings of his father's restless spirit, and he continued to walk over the snowy hills of Hydra, until he was close enough to the fortress to cause the keepers of its gates to become disturbed by the strange monk approaching, hooded and cloaked in black rags that blew in the wind, and raised the drawbridge to prevent him crossing the moat. He came and stood on his side of the moat, before the drawbridge, and one of the Hydran gatekeepers called out to him, 'laremad'gverk!' Michael heard a continued chorus of agitated Hydran voices on the wall, as he ignored the foul speech of the enemy and continued to approach the moat.

He could not cross over the water and reach the gate by foot, so he plunged into the moat and swam across to the raised drawbridge. He struggled for a moment in the moat, because his leg became tangled in some chains that lay there among dumped refuse and the dead remains of men and livestock. In his moment of delay, he heard arrows whistle down at him from the wall of the fortress, and cut into the water. One arrow struck him in the leg, but he pulled it from the wound, which closed and healed with great rapidity. But the arrows did not trouble him, for he saw a serpent's eye fast approaching beneath the water, and he did not wish to become imprisoned in the belly of such a creature, for that might delay him. And such a delay might be long enough to see his terrible Harvester complete its search, and, tearing open the serpent, find him.

So he rose out of the moat and came onto the dirt at the foot of the battle-scarred fortress, so that he was facing the withdrawn drawbridge. He looked up, and, focusing his hand and his mind, quickly made a sphere of fire that was sufficient to destroy the drawbridge and the gate behind it, when thrown against the wood. After he had accomplished this act of militarised sorcery, he could hear, by their voices, that the Hydran soldiers were in a frenzy of confusion and terror, and this brought great pleasure to Michael's heart, for he knew that he was inflicting a familiar fate, on them, that so many Rose soldiers had witnessed when they fell in battle with the Hydran foe. Michael knew that they would not grant him passage to the Sephric prince, whom he intended to assassinate, and would sacrifice their own lives in service of such a monster, which was as a god to them. So he knew that they would all try to stop his passage, and they would all need to be put to the sword.

Through the burned doors, he entered into the hall of the great keep, which was filled with Hydran warriors. And, drawing his blade, he hewed relentlessly, without sight and mind, and carved a path through them, leaving many bloodied corpses behind him along the stone floor. Only the body seemed to carry out the dark deed, and Michael felt no responsibility, even as he watched his hand drive the sword through men's heads and hearts, and there was so much butchery that the corridors flowed with Hydran blood. He proceeded up the stairs, hewing many more of the wicked soldiers dead as he passed, until he reached a great barrack chamber and nearly a hundred men converged on him. All of the soldiers in the fortress came, and were beheaded or hewn without seeming to deal any injury to their target, until it seemed as if all the blood that Hydra had planned to shed across a vast field of battle had prematurely flowed onto a barrack floor. The massacre in the fortress created the most unsightly grave that an army can achieve, but it gave endless satisfaction, to Michael, to see these sore days dawn for Hydra. At last, there was a terrible Hydran defeat, witnessed in their own homeland, as bloody as the worst days the Rose had suffered.

When he had slain all the foes in the large barrack chamber, Michael found no more Hydran soldiers in fortress, and this disappointed him, for the sight of them in pieces, and the blood flowing from them across the stone floors, had greatly pleased him. He had put the whole guard to the sword, and the fortress was empty of life. These were the dreadful images and sounds that he wanted to recreate, over and over again, for his endless satisfaction, because it fed the void inside him. It was the same void that had been carved out, inside, when he lost his home, and could never be filled by anything but more death, destruction and fire. All the tenderness within Michael's heart seemed to have perished, with the development of his infinite hatred of the Sephrics and their realm. He would seek them, and kill them, and, when they were all dead, he would suffer worst, because nothing would be able to feed the mouth of the void, and the void would expand and devour him instead. It would find him, and it would take him, and he would regret everything. He would wish that he had never done any of these deeds he revelled in.

Michael knew that Draco the Cruel was near, as though he could hear the pernicious thoughts of the demon inhabiting the Sephric prince, and he believed that he knew the target's precise location atop the keep, so that he could faster find him. He ascended the staircase that accessed the top, and saw the grey clouds above, but was struck by a poisoned arrow, that had been made with great skill, through his back. It entered his heart, and he was shocked to discover that he lacked immunity to its effects. As he slowed, he regretted the rage that had taken him and driven him, without sight or mind, through the corridors and chambers, slaying all in his path. If he had approached the top of the keep carefully, and been prepared for the

157

prince with his accursed hand filled with red flames, then the outcome of his encounter with Draco might have been more fortunate.

Instead, Michael was slow, and he saw only a blur coming at him, but he knew that it was certainly a pale-skinned and dark-haired noble, surely a Sephric prince, who was coming to kill him. His height was greater than the Sephric general Kraide, or the sorcerer Nefarion, and he was certainly a greater son, invested with the greatest amount of the malevolent and destructive Sephric power. He might even have been a stronger adversary than the evil king Hardrad. None, save Hardrad himself, could hitherto have emerged as a challenger to the great fighting skill and physical might of Draco. Yet, the son may have been even stronger than his father, for Draco was known as Hydra's greatest huntsman, and he had a cursed bow that delivered enchanted arrows to its targets, and an arm so strong to pull the string, that possibly no one but he could use this weapon in combat.

Now Michael manifested some fire, by the sorcery of his hands, but it was weak, and it was not enough to break the prince, even though the prince wore little armour. Draco's pride and confidence in his physical strength was expressed in his lack of armour, for he was crowned and caped, and he wore rich garments adorned with the symbols of his house. These details were clear to Michael, as he dropped his sword, for he fell to his knees under the draining effects of the arrow, numbed and confused in body and mind. He felt that he had witnessed the final failure of the powers of Guidonis. Where had the monk been, to allow him to be so weak? The prince came very close to him, and looked down at him, gloating over his pitiful prey. The prince uttered some mocking Hydran expression, which sounded as nothing more than a grotesque grunt to Michael's ears, but he did not pay much attention, for he was speaking his own words in reaction to the outcome of his short confrontation with the lord of the dark fortress.

'Guidonis! Your wisdom!' the defeated assassin demanded, 'is this not a quest of three?' and he also looked for the light of his sister, which he knew could tear through all the curtains of shadow and offer him clarity in this moment of confusion, but he could not find that either. 'Berenice!' he shouted, knowing that his defeat was at hand, and he was confused and disappointed at the failure of his mentor, Guidonis. The heretic could not tolerate this outcome, and Michael believed that Guidonis was an incredible being capable of attaining anything he set out to accomplish. Why, now, did he fail? It was surely something to do with the inner machinations of the quest's triad of souls. Without absolute simultaneity of ambition in the three preselected souls, to ultimately complete the quest, the enchantments of the body of Michael would be suspended. One of those three in the coalition had faulted. And it was neither he nor Guidonis. He knew that he must accept this momentary defeat, but he would return to complete the quest, later. His immediate mission should be to find the answer to this riddle, after escaping this foolish battle with Draco.

He tried to back away from the prince, to escape the arena of the confrontation, and fall from the battlements into the moat, so that he could somehow flee, but the prince was already upon him. As Draco gloated over his victim, the prince drew a strange blade adorned with Hydran glyphs, and put it to the neck of the bettered killer, severing Michael's head, which still stared perilously into the sinister glow of its liberator's eyes. Michael was defeated, but still had no reason to fear the prince. Only the Harvester, which was still a three day march away from him, could harm him. No damage done to the body could destroy the triad of the quest, and as long as some remnant of the original coalition existed, the body would find ways to survive any kind of harm. Not even the corrosive torments inside the belly of the giant serpent of the moat could undo the body, so powerful were the enchantments of Guidonis.

And the belly of the snake in the moat was Michael's next destination, because the prince cut him into many pieces and threw them all from the battlements. All of this was a blur to the astral entity of Michael inside the body, and his spirit came free, manifesting as a ghost like his two allies, so that he had an experience like a pair of floating eyes, liberated from these pieces of flesh, as the serpent in the water consumed them. He descended, again, into the familiar Dark Plane, which was the illusory realm of his fold, as he faded out of the world of the quest. Through a strange black fog, he waded, pursued by the two ghosts of his alliance. Now, he regained his purpose in the shadows, and knew that he had to find the answer to the aforementioned riddle. Which of them had forsaken the quest? Which of them had forsaken the mission to ruin the House of Sephric?

VIII. WE ARE OUR OWN PRISONS

Michael took counsel with Guidonis and spoke long with him, there in the Dark Plane, asking how it had come to pass that Draco had slain the body integral to the quest. Because they both disapproved of her counsel, Berenice was not present during this exchange, for Guidonis had dispatched her away from them, so that all three of them would not be found together, and be vulnerable to the sudden return of the body's Harvester. If they had not chosen to exclude Berenice from the discussion, they would probably be eaten together, and thence purged from their wandering state between life and death. In the Dark Plane, the veil between the living and the dead is very thin, and it was a dangerous place for the members of this coalition to dwell, because the Undergrave and its agents were increasingly hungry for the souls of the heretic Guidonis and his pupil.

They travelled for many miles in caverns of ice, in search of a safe place, until they found a refuge that was devoid of the presence of any other restless, mourning spirits. By the sorcery of their minds and hands, they bent the rock, stone and ice and created a safe place to reside in, to shield them from the Harvester as it pursued them. Finally, they were inside a hollow, and they remained there, mustering all the deadliest forms of witchcraft to obey them, and readying their minds and their hands for the coming battle with the agent of their doom.

'Our main concern, for now, is the shadow being seeking our doom,' Guidonis said, 'it is a herald of evil. Do not regard it as a maker of balance in the world, as some believe their reapers to be. They are demons, and their very presence in the world is worse heresy than the act that released them. By our righteous science, we seek to mend ills. We do not create them. And all the heresy that we have done is the lesser of two evils. The Sephrics must be defeated, and we are their reapers, and we are more righteous than the vacuous being pursuing us.'

'What must be done to heal the body?' Michael asked.

'It is being restored now, for it passed through the body of the serpent of the moat, and is now lost somewhere in the canal on the west of Draco's Fortress. From the river on the west of Hydra, the body will arise and return to battle against Draco, when its time comes. But I am not sure of the nature of the body's weakness. My mind is focused upon the Harvester. I sense a great deal of fear and doubt in your sister, Berenice, and I believe that she is possibly the source of this weakness. Whether she ought to be convinced, again, of the righteousness of our cause, as I once convinced you, or if she is better exorcised from our coalition, I do not know.'

'How might she be exorcised from our alliance? Is she not a necessary ally, as I believed her to be?'

'I believe that she might be losing faith in the quest,' Guidonis said, 'if she does, then we will see if the body is stronger without her. We may yet form a coalition of two. Your power has grown, Michael. Ever since you gained the powers of fire, I believed that you were gaining similar capabilities to mine. You will soon be powerful enough, so that you and I are sufficient counterweights, and we will be able to cohabit in the body without the aid of your sister. Such an alliance would be better suited to this quest.'

'But the quest is stronger in a coalition of three, which was a ritual necessity. Berenice provides moral guidance, and has often restrained how far the quest could take us. It may oft have seemed a hindrance, but it was also an important part of the righteousness of the quest, when it began.'

'The exercise of such restraint has proven to be more troublesome than useful. We are bound to an errand coldblooded and terrible. Hatred of your enemy, not the love your kin, is the only thing that may direct you. A series of dark deeds, foul and unsightly, must be done, and they are necessary. It is incumbent upon all beings in the quest to consent to slay the Sephrics and bring Hydra to its end. It is not something that a foolish young woman is capable of understanding. The whole world is bound to the outcome of this quest, and its accomplishment will mark the triumph of good over evil in the world, even if our methods are seemingly wicked.'

'Then we must speak to Berenice, in order to exorcise her,' Michael decided.

'Of course. Together, we must convince her that the quest must be finished, even if we appear to have already bought the safety of Rose. The House of Sephric cannot be allowed to recuperate and return to Rose, to attack its people again. Furthermore, the body cannot linger in this world. It must accomplish its task as soon as possible, to bring an end to its purpose in the world. It would be a tragic error for the body to be lost, and for the House of Sephric to continue to control its warlike nation. Once the quest is over, the souls of yourself and Berenice may be at rest, for their purpose will be complete. That is what you seek, is it not?'

'I seek the safety of Rose, and the accomplishment of Hydra's destruction. Of course, my own fate is irrelevant. It was always irrelevant. I made my choice, the moment I was bound to this errand. There was never any turning back from my fate. My sister will follow us, or she will leave, and we will grow into a stronger coalition of two, unending, to provide eternal security to Rose.'

'If it is needed, and if it is your wish, the body may be perpetuated as an eternal silent guardian for all the decency in the world. It will serve as the destroyer of evil. I share your design. But, before we confront Berenice's disloyalty and the wavering of her purpose, we must be certain that we have security from the Harvester,' Guidonis concluded. And he sensed the coming of that being, and said, 'beyond the ice! It approaches! Make ready all the magic your hands can unleash, for a great battle is near!'

The seal of their confinement in ice and stone broke asunder, and a titanic entity drove through the breach, to prey upon them. But each of them saw a different physical form in the space occupied by the spectre. To Guidonis, it was a monstrous, blind hunchback, drooling as if it was drained of all sentience, and moving clumsily, as if it was a hulking shell of rotting flesh, lacking a soul of its own, and relentlessly seeking to compensate by devouring one of these two disembodied beings. Yet, to Michael, it was a hulking mass of black muscle with human and animal characteristics, like a giant ape, but it had pale eyes gleaming brighter than a Sephric's, and its head was crowned with two long sharp objects like a gazelle's horns or a rabbit's ears. Certainly, it must have been in two places at once, for both of the sorcerers now attacked different locations, but all seemed to be at war with the same entity, projecting two illusions.

Simultaneously, they summoned the ice to slow it, and the dash of the rabbit creature and the lumber of the hunchback were both slowed, so that the unified entity froze but it retained both of its appearances. Then, they summoned a terrible fire, and it funnelled from their palms, so powerfully that it looked as if it had been breathed from the mouth of a dragon, and the fearsome roar of the fire rivalled the sounds of a dragon, also. Yet, despite the storm of flame that was sent against the vacuous being, it only succeeded in counteracting the effect of the ice, and the Harvester's speed was restored. Again, it marched in their pursuit, so that they had to stay on the move around the hollow, with a cautious step, lest they stumble on the icy floor.

Again, they called to the ice, so that sharp white crystals rose up against the creature and tried to form a prison for it, but the ever-pursuing shadow shattered this barrier and was not slowed, because it was a warrior unassailable as the foundations of the earth.

'How much longer?' Michael demanded, when they had their backs to the hollow's edge, 'when will the body be ready? We must fly from this devilry, by taking to the skies. The winged mount circles!'

Indeed, the great bat, which had belonged to Nefarion, but had changed its allegiance so that it could serve a greater sorcerer, was aware of the battle with the Harvester, and it was keen to deliver the body from its peril. Some part of the bat's being was reaching through, into the Dark Plane, in search of its master, and there was an occasional ripple of water and a flutter of wings that pierced through into the illusory fortress of ice wherein the disembodied beings fought their Harvester, in wait of the body's recovery. Bound to the body and the quest, the bat was circling above the western river of Hydra, in relentless search of the bones of its waking master. The faithful creature knew that he would rise up from the river, again, returned to the unassailable body, hooded and cloaked in the ragged black veils of the Dark Plane, and he would be armed with a new sword, forged by the raw and heretical sorcery of Guidonis. He would claim it, and wield it to finish the quest.

'The body nears its recovery! It will be done ere the sun rises. Look to the dark wings! Look to the sword!' Guidonis said, and great hope was returned to Michael's heart, when he saw a flaming sword in the Dark

Plane. The expression had been no mere metaphor. Michael was destined to become one with this sword, and use it to unlock this destiny. It was a sword newly appointed to him in the quest, by the wisdom and magic of Guidonis, and it needed only his hand on its hilt to return him to the body, and the sword to the hand of the body.

Michael possessed immediate knowledge that the sword was certainly one of the keys to the accomplishment of the quest, for the smallest exposure to its fiery blade would be deadly to the flesh of the Sephrics and their servants. He could not reach the sword, because he was soon in the hands of the tall Harvester, and it lifted him to lower him into the dark abyss of its mouth. As he descended and was surrounded by sharp teeth, which appeared as a giant cat's, he resisted the creature's grasp with all the strength he could muster. He focused his mind on the reality, knowing that the experience was but an illusory expression of the climactic metaphysical confrontation with the punitive Harvester of his lost soul, and that it was by his soul's focus and will, not an illusion of bodily strength, that he would prevail. But the Harvester's proximity was real, and even his strongest spiritual concentration could not counter its grasp.

Guidonis liberated Michael from the Harvester, as he diverted it away by approaching the flaming sword, in an attempt to make the creature believe that his intent was to claim the weapon and use it for himself. Knowing the importance of the sword, the creature turned and tried to pursue Gudionis, and dropped Michael to the ground.

'Run! We must fly! We cannot combat this creature!' Guidonis warned Michael, and they used magic to shatter a path through the ice and stone, and fled the Harvester.

'What hope is there of prevail by our flight?' Michael asked, as they fled.

'We must find the source of this weakness! It is necessary that we must find your young sister, and exorcise this weakness and disloyalty from the stupid girl!'

Michael was no longer concerned for his sister's fate, so he was supportive of the intentions of Guidonis. Certainly, her treatment meant nothing, for the only meaningful thing now would be the accomplishment of the quest. The coalition of two used their sorcery, and created walls of ice and stone to slow the advance of the Harvester, but they knew that it could not be delayed for long. The weakness of the covenant of the body was strengthening and emboldening the creature. It was certain to devour both of them, unless they could soon exorcise the weakness that was breaking the covenant.

So, in another hollow of ice, they met up with Berenice, and she was standing, and seemed strong and righteous, as she had been whenever Michael had last taken counsel with her. She was still a bright and beautiful figure to behold, even in the hour of the greatest peril. However, Michael no longer had any care for her. Though strong she may have been in her morals, and though a beacon of certain decency, she was surely arrogant, and she had forsaken the quest. Her pride was damaging the hopes of the oppressed, eliminating the chances of the Rose and all the other weak nations to achieve their liberation from the Sephric evil. The stakes were too high for individual concerns, even over damnation in hell, to intervene. Despite her light and beauty, she had certainly become an agent of ills, and she had to be exorcised from the alliance.

'You seem agitated,' she said to them, 'need I remind you that your quest has achieved everything necessary, already. You have already taken off the claws of the Hydran beast. Without their chief general and sorcerer, they have been without the means to attack Rose again. They would never oppress this country again. Yet you are still fixated on taking off the beast's head. You would still persist in this aggression, even if, in destroying their house, you inherit the place of the beast. Evil necessarily inhabits the world. When an attempt is made to purge it utterly, then whosoever embarks on this quest will inherit its place. Already, you thirst for blood. You know of what I speak. The void within, ever hungering. Ever unsatisfied. A void carved out inside you by acts of unforgivable original evil, passed on with the tragedy of creation, cursed to plague the living and the dead, forever. This void craves to see suffering. Terrible suffering. This void is malice. When it manifests agency, it becomes the thing that we know as evil. And evil is real. It is no mere abstract. Malice and ill will are realities, and you have seen them, and they are a necessary part of existence, ever since the original tragedies and falls that happened in creation, but I do not wish to be a part of this coalition any longer. You fight evil, but, as you triumph, so evil will find its new host in you!'

'Listen to yourself!' Guidonis retorted, 'you are so bloated with pride that you cannot understand the nature of the sacrifice. Michael has offered himself up as a sacrifice. He cares not for what awaits. He has even said that he would face the torments of Hades if it means he denies evil the opportunity to violate and torture his people and other innocents in the world again. Heretics, we may be! And, by our heresy, many are saved from worse crimes. The body may die a thousand deaths, but that doesn't

172

matter. It is better that one should die a thousand times, than that a thousand should die once! It is better that one should face eternal punishment, than that punishment be dealt eternal upon all!'

'Michael!' Berenice said, 'I am your sister! The one you swore to avenge! Don't you know your own sister? What of your father, who forsook you, but loved you again when you had avenged him at the Battle of the Three Stairs? You ignored this, because you were blinded by the deception of Guidonis. This heretic has deceived you. When you first saw him, you had thoughts that he had his own ulterior ambition and would not share it with you. You felt that he was using you. That you were part of some vile experiment. I see his mind now! You were right from the beginning! Guidonis is evil!'

'No!' Michael shouted in protest at her words, and he hurled a sphere of fire at her image, but it passed through her, for she was not real. 'Guidonis is like a father to me! He has given me purpose and life! My own father has become nothing but a wandering shadow, weeping like a girl! I have no respect for the one who called himself my father before. I have no respect for you, a self-infatuated and treacherous harpy! You think yourself an angel, but there are probably Sephric women who are destined to be killed by the flaming blade that I will soon acquire, and they are surely as

173

fair in form as you. Family? Love? It is all a deception! You are nothing but a lie! Get out! Get out of this iron pact, and weep! There is no place for weakness in the quest. The road is long, and I know that fell deeds, wrath, and fire wait! Never, shall I stop. Not until the home of the Sephrics is engulfed in flame, and I see the slain corpses of the Hydran monarchs Hardrad and Heldra, bloodied and burned with more pain and destruction than everything they wreaked upon the world, in the ashes of their own filthy lair. These Sephrics must suffer everything they did to the world, tenfold.'

'Then it is done,' Guidonis said, and Berenice fell to her knees before them, and her appearance seemed to become dull. She trembled, as if she was very cold among the illusory prison of ice. 'You foolish girl,' Guidonis continued, 'you have not been liberated from anything, by forsaking and leaving our coalition. You will remain here, forever. You will weep, and your tears will strengthen the prison of ice that contains you. The Harvester will not penetrate this chamber, for it contains this weeping woman, and her constant tears make certain that nothing can enter. May the Harvester forever stare at you though the ice and haunt you, for its form will be as all your fears incarnate!'

It was done in accord with the curse of Guidonis, and she wept for a long time. She wept in the chamber, and the covenant of two did not look back or have any pity, as they opened the wall of ice, sealing it behind them as they escaped, and the Harvester did not pursue the two dark and violent beings as they left the chamber, for it had a greater desire to devour the weeping woman. Her own darkness was now more terrible than Michael's, and it had a stronger gravity for the Harvester. The Harvester did not pursue the heretics, and circled the chamber of ice instead, but it was never able to break it, because the woman's cold tears only froze, and made the ice forever impenetrable. Thus did the Harvester cease to hunt the heretics, and they were able to go on with their quest.

'With this new coalition of two, nothing will oppose us!' Michael said to Guidonis, as his triumphal hand took the flaming sword, and he swore that he would use it to pierce every remaining black heart of the Sephric House.

And so the body rose up again, in black ragged robes, from the waters of the eastern river, and was claimed by the winged mount in the night. The assassin carried a flaming sword, and had reconstituted strength and purpose. When the body returned to fight against the prince of the Hydran fortress, Draco the Cruel knew that it was the same assassin, but it was also changed. The flaming sword hurt the prince's eyes, even to look at, for he knew that it was made solely for the destruction of his whole house. Quite wisely, he had sent his wife, Princess Gorra, away to safety in a mountain sanctuary to the north. This was done for fear that the assassin might catch her and kill her, for she was a Sephric princess capable of bearing children, and the assassin surely intended to destroy the Sephric line, thus making her a high-value target.

IX. OMEN OF THE DEAD PRINCE

The fortress bore many signs of damage, and was burned inside, and the prince had wounds too. Because his soldiers had been slaughtered by the mysterious assassin, he had been caught in a battle that left him no choice than to singlehandedly repel an attack by the free men of Westcross, who were seeking to exploit the mysterious destruction of his castle guard as an opportunity to kill him. Fallen Westcross soldiers were strewn around, and most had been decapitated. Others had been thrown into the moat, to be food for the serpent in residence there. The moat had claimed the bones of many an enemy of Hydra, and only the indestructible Rose assassin had risen from its fell water alive.

Draco fired an enchanted arrow at Michael, who caught it in his hand, and lit it with his sword's flame. Then, he threw it with great strength, and it bolted back at its owner with the same power as there had been in its dispatch. Now, the prince's blade cut the arrow and it did not touch him, but he did not fire any other arrows at the assassin. The prince waited and held a sword out in confrontation. Eager to obtain revenge for the pain of his earlier destruction, Michael came and cut the prince's sword blunt with his own fiery weapon, before stabbing into the heart of Draco with the flaming

177

blade. However, the prince laughed mockingly, and the fire of the sword diminished, to the astonishment of Michael. It seemed, in this moment, as though the promises of this sword were a deception. He had been certain that it was appointed to him so that he could kill the Sephrics. And now it was failing him? At that juncture, the prince tried to cut the assassin with a dagger he took from his belt, even while his own body was impaled, and was confused when he saw that he could not harm the flesh of Michael. Somehow, this assassin had returned with even more terrible power than had been evident before, and this struck fear and doubt into the Sephric, although he did not seem to lose any of the tenacity he had displayed in every moment Michael had battled him. The prince was so tenacious that he had defended his fortress, alone, and slain an entire army of Westcross invaders from the west.

From the wound of his chest, all seven serpents of the Hydran lord's internal frame finally emerged in their fullest aggression, and Draco projected them relentlessly, his own eyes now containing a fiery look of outrage he had never shown before. The champion's demonic allies lifted Michael into the air and drove their fangs into his body, but they did not deter him. He grasped the long black hair of the champion, propelling himself closer to the vicious head, and he plunged his sword directly through the mouth and down the gullet of the pale human frame, to reach the heart of the dragon contained within. Instead, the suction of the flesh almost took the sword from Michael's hand, and he was forced to pull it with great exertion from the prince's neck. With his sword now in his hand again, Michael grabbed the champion by his muscular neck and hacked each of the serpents from the point of their projection at the belly, until all but three were all thrown down into the pool of the fallen prince's blood. The prince collapsed with his last three allies and they tried to carry his snarling body away, but Michael crushed the chest with his boot and cut off the remaining snakes by stabbing again at the monstrous chest wound the dragon's heads had emerged from.

Michael knew his body was stronger than the prince's, and he would not suffer the Sephric son to live a moment longer. He pulled his sword from the prince's heart, and swung it with such strength that the dark-haired Sephric head was cleanly severed and thudded instantly against the stone. The bleeding body collapsed beside it, in defeat. Michael revelled as he lifted the head and approached the edge of the fortress and looked down to the moat and the west, where the lands no longer had anything to fear from their former oppressor.

The sun was rising, but the bat was still near, and the shapes of men and horses were coming in from the west, from the distant land of Westcross. They saw, and were surely haunted by, the ragged black-robed figure between the battlements, holding a severed head speckled with dark blood, with dark hair and pale eyes. And they were also disturbed by the bat they saw circling against the red dawn. They were terrified, when the head fell down into the water and was swallowed by a giant serpent, and the robed foreign assassin called the bat to him. And he rode away on the bat, so that it took him away from the rising sun. He was delivered a great distance to the west, but was taken out of the sight of the approaching Westcross soldiers.

Guidonis assured Michael, 'as Draco was assassinated, so too will the whole Sephric House be put to the sword, if you retain your faith in the quest, where your sister was unable.'

Michael promised his tutor, 'I surrender myself to the quest of vengeance. I am an agent of the doom of the House of Sephric and the nation of Hydra. I care not for what happens to my own soul after death anymore!' and he dismounted the bat, and went into hiding so that the Westcross armies would not try to investigate the causes of Draco's defeat, and search for the assassin. Although Michael retained great sympathy for the free men of the world, who continued to war against Hydra with mortal weapons, and probably mistakenly praised the assassin as a mysterious angel of light, he knew that he could never rejoin them. Despite knowing that he would be greatly applauded, if ever he should tell these mortals of his quest, he was determined not to share his dark deeds or the nature of his heresy with them. To present a monstrous and irredeemable assassin as the new ideal of a hero would be dangerous, for they might follow him to certain ruin, in awe of him, and fall into darkness too, becoming like the accursed realm of Hydra in the end. If any soul had to perish in undeserved hellfire, it had to be the soul of Michael. He had made this choice, and had surrendered to fire and destruction, so that he could see it spread into Hydra to punish its own kindlers. The ones who birthed this terrible inferno of war would suffer the worst from it. It was only a fulfilment of cosmic justice.

There would, perhaps, be monsters occupying the shapes of men, women and children, of many apparent ages, sustaining the Sephric House, Michael knew. But they would be only a collection of illusory appearances to maintain the legitimacy of an army of monsters. Those smaller entities would undoubtedly grow up into more generals and sorcerers for the evil nation, if he did not prevent them. Those women would be as tenacious as the men, and would give birth to countless more of the murderous Sephric rulers. It was necessary, for the good of the quest, to find the Sephric mountain strongholds, where they cowered, and massacre them. It was necessary to keep them deep in their sanctuaries, cowering, while the armies of Hydra's many enemies poured into their lands to pillage and burn, and slaughter their accursed soldiers until their whole realm was undone.

The Prince of Hydra was dead. It was the signal. Hydra's doors were open, and her enemies were invited to witness her demise. It was probably unnecessary that Michael should personally do the dark deeds of killing off all the lesser Sephrics, as the incoming armies of Hydra's enemies, too numerous to count, would surely do it instead. So, instead, Michael focused all his efforts on travelling to the Sephric home to kill Hardrad. He had achieved the full wisdom of Guidonis, and had awareness of all the darkest places of the world, so he knew where to find the monster at last.

X. BLOOD OF EVIL

Michael set out, at last, for the great Castle of Sephric, the ancient home of the Sephric family, which had served them for countless generations, and was the present home of the king of Hydra. Tales abounded that, of the whole Sephric House, only King Hardrad was yet to be mysteriously killed, and he presently cowered in his castle, in the hopes of somehow restoring his house and re-forging his tyrannical kingdom. Only with the fiery end of the king of Hydra, could his house be finally destroyed, his kingdom fall, and evil be purged from the land.

The relentless wandering assassin had learned that he was in this last phase of his quest, when he dismounted near an expeditionary Rose military camp near the ruins of the fortress of the fallen prince Draco, avoiding the fearful eyes of the Rose soldiers, who would easily mistake him and his mount for demons. In some part of the camp, he had listened to the conversations of the soldiers and their leaders. Many of the exchanges between the men in the camp revealed the nature of the final phase of the Rose campaign and the closeness of Hydra to its final defeat. "The problem," the leader of a host of Rose had said, "is the chance that Hardrad will flee to some distant land or a hideout that we cannot enter. There, he might be able to recuperate and save his realm from utter ruin. This is why we must strike soon. But the siege of the Castle of Sephric will be lengthy, because it is manned by a vast army, and it is likely that Hardrad has made preparations to evacuate to someplace safe."

So, leaving that encampment of valiant invaders, Michael had found his winged mount again and flown many miles, watching the advance of the Rose army, until he saw Castle Sephric, which was a tall square wall of dark grey stone enclosing many strong buildings, and had a well-fortified keep at its centre, and a high tower with a pinnacle that stood atop the keep. Michael did not fly too close to the Hydran watchmen on his winged mount, through fear of being seen by them, and so he instead travelled to a river that joined to the moat. He dismounted the bat as it continued to fly, and fell into the river, so that its currents carried him into the moat of the castle, where he stayed beneath the water to avoid being seen, and swam under the main wall, by way of the murky water.

He was able to reach behind the main wall, he entered the city, and he rose up at some rear part of the castle's interior, which was not accessible near the gate, and so there were few Hydran defenders there. He needed slay only three patrolling guardsmen before he reached the gateway of the great hall, which was inside the main keep, and he threw open the strong wooden doors, entering the royal palace unopposed. At this time, he heard the battle horns of the besieging army, the cries of men dying, and the perilous sounds of the siege machines cracking against stone. The brave men of Rose had reached the walls, and they were going into battle against the dark castle with no fear of the poisoned and cursed arrows of Hydra or the sleepless evils waiting for confrontation in the fortress. He remembered his own days of mortality, and it made him eager to complete his quest quickly, to prevent more Rose soldiers from suffering torturous misfortunes in battle against the power of the Sephrics.

He was shocked by the interior's magnificence. At first, he thought the ornate walls had surely once belonged to some to some other civilisation, but it was the accursed many-headed serpent whose symbol had been so perfectly carved into the stone. In all of Hydra, he had so far seen only ugly fortresses, expressive of a people whose only religion was war. These royal places were clearly designed to impress, and to build the godly image of the Sephrics, as lords over mankind. But the place was not without a guard of equally awesome perfection, for an arrow burning with a bright red flame whistled towards him, and struck him in the chest, aided by an oral curse of apocalyptic intonations. His pain was numbed by his fury, and Michael pulled the bloody stick of wood from his healing chest, without even the slightest expression of discomfort, and threw the object with such force that it struck its owner through the eye, and he fell from the balcony, with blood gushing from his skull.

At the same balcony where Hardrad had surely made loud promises of conquest to the court of Hydra, one of his own soldiers had now fallen. The place was defended by the feared Royal Guards, gigantic warriors whose sorcery-aided arrows were said to be capable of killing a man at any distance. But Michael was a hooded creature of another world, and already responsible for killing the feared Prince of Hydra. He had already assailed their champion, so he had no fear of them or their disgraced ruler, whose armies and walls were falling all about him.

Michael went to the steps on his right, and began to ascend the staircase that took him to the higher level of the castle. The staircase, too, was made of very ornately carved and polished stone, with gargoyles and serpentine statues resting atop its columns. The sinister beauty of the place convinced Michael of its doom. It had to all be destroyed. Evil was present in its very foundations. For all of its richness and its past, it was the Hydran past. It was the history of the Sephrics. No Rose could tolerate such a dark place to continue standing. He could feel the ground shake with the force of the siege machines that were attacking the castle, and was certain that the

Rose meant not to enter the fortress at all. They would prefer to tear it all down with their machines, by hurling spheres of stone and flame against it. Knowing that it would aid the besiegers, Michael used his own powers of sorcery to manifest and spread fire onto the tapestries, curtains and carpets. Although these were very royal adornments in the castle, and he believed that they were beautiful, the only use he could see for them was to speed to demise of Hydra, and there could be no hindering the righteous flames as they consumed everything, helping to bring doom upon Hardrad's kingdom.

As Michael approached a higher level of the castle in his search for Hardrad, two of the ruler's mightiest swordsmen in black garb intercepted him. They were tall and strong of frame, wielding swords with such strength that they could have cut through several men and horses in the battlefield. But Michael's flesh was too strong for them to destroy. One of these guards, Michael slew by slicing through the neck and casting him down into the hall. The other, he beheaded, and kicked the twitching body out of his path. He left their bloody heaps behind him, and proceeded to find their master.

The scent of spilled Hydran blood and the smoke from the burning Hydran banners and tapestries filled him with confidence that the doom of Hydra was near, and he smashed through a wooden door that led him to a last great stairway. From here, he found the stone floor at the top of the keep, and the High Tower of the Hydran king.

His heart raced and his eyes widened as he found the monster he sought to destroy. Standing before the door to the High Tower, he found his most terrible adversary. He knew it was the evil ruler Hardrad, because he was the largest and most muscular of any Sephric he had encountered. He was the most powerful opponent he had faced. A truly a terrifying adversary, double in height to a common man, and with hands strong enough to lift whole bodies and break them apart with the smallest effort. The stone of his fortress rumbled with his footsteps as he approached Michael. Hardrad had been waiting to do battle with the assassin. His furious eyes were filled with malice so intense they seemed like windows into the furnaces of the Undergrave. His beard and hair were as black as the eternal void of death, his skin as white as the iciest wastes of his realm. There he stood at the door of the High Tower, between two great pillars of stone, knowing he was a warrior strong enough to cut whole armies down by his own hand.

He made a Hydran battle cry, and did not speak again, for he towered over Michael in his black armour as he stood before the high tower, and delivered a strong blow downward at the assassin with his massive sword.

The sword was black, and it was reinforced with some ancient curse, which troubled Michael, for he half expected it to shatter his own blade. But Guidonis would avail him through the worst hardships, even in battle against the towering warrior king of Hydra. Michael's knowledge that the king was the greatest warrior of Hydra made him fear his adversary. And he had not truly been afraid since the times of confusion at the start of the quest.

Hardrad's armour soon proved impenetrable, for it was aided by magic equal to the curses driving the sword of Michael. His armour had guards at the joints of each limb to prevent dismemberment. The only exposed part was at the back. Some strapping was present there. Each time Michael moved in close to the monster's back, Hardrad would butt him with his iron fists or elbows, which propelled spikes capable of impaling a normal man. Eventually, Michael resorted to use enchanted fire from his hands to cook the king in his armour. He released it, and the armour gradually increased in temperature. Each time the king struck him with his armoured fists, their contact was intensely hot, so Michael knew his strategy was beginning to work.

After much time using projectiles of fire to heat Hardrad's armour, the king's flesh began to cook. But because he was so confident of his power,

Hardrad was not hesitant to remove the armour, and when he had discarded it the immensely strong torso possessed much greater agility. But Michael could now strike the king's arms successfully, to initiate combat with the creature inhabiting his false form. Even without the armour, the immense arms were as thick as men, and Michael was unsuccessful in his attempts to simply slash them from his body. Such attempts created no more than repeated scars and scratches against the giant's body. Although he could cut deep, it would take far too many strikes to accomplish anything close to dismemberment, and the monster would surely anticipate it. Hardrad was just too mighty to be defeated in the manner of any other son of the House of Sephric.

Finally, Michael used his own superior agility to move in close enough to Hardrad to provoke a strike from the king's immense fist. As soon as the fist had passed him, he stabbed into the arm as deep as possible, so that he felt it cut the bone, and climbed up onto the giant's limb to complete the amputation. He levered the sword around the entire arm from the point of the bone, shearing the limb off by slicing through all of the muscle surrounding that centre. As he did so, he kicked Hardrad's head repeatedly to keep the monster distracted enough to allow the completion of the act of strategic amputation. When the assassin's work was done, he dropped down onto the blood-splattered stone. And the immensely powerful arm of the king, now completely severed, came down with him. Blood poured from the massive stump left by the amputation, and flowed across the stone until a great dark pool covered the whole fortification. With his remaining arm, Hardrad took hold of Michael's body and threw him with tremendous force to the battlements, in the hope of seeing him tumble down to his impalement on the spears his besieging countrymen.

The one-armed titan approached the assassin with thundering footsteps and struck at him with his sword. Michael leapt from the path of the blade, which shattered the stone where he had rested. The assassin dived under the king and cut the tendon at each heel like thick ropes. This decisive action immobilised Hardrad's body, and Michael was then able to sheer off the remaining arm of the kneeling king before it could grasp him, with all the same efficacy as before.

Hardrad still wielded a titanic and strong body, but he was without arms, so his sword was abandoned. Each stump released three vicious serpents to serve as his new weapons. Two from each arm became offensive limbs to help increase the body's speed like a spider. One from each arm was held high and dived down at Michael, who fought them back with his sword. These were stronger serpents than the others Michael had battled, but by investing greater strength he was able to dismember the two assailing projections from the mighty muscles of the torso. The remaining four visible serpents abandoned their place as additional legs, becoming offensive instead. The king's footsteps still rumbled, and his eyes were like balls of fire as his bony head bent down in hatred at his enemy, accompanied by the four hissing serpents. He still stood at twice Michael's height, but he was not able to use his sword any longer, for his fighting arms had both been severed. Knowing that the sword might now serve his own purposes, Michael took it and thrust it into the belly of the king. It pierced deep into his stomach, and his innards and blood fell as Michael twisted the weapon inside him, until Hardrad had been utterly sliced in half at the waist.

With Hardrad's lower body now severed, his upper torso now continued the battle. It stood shorter than Michael. His bloody eyes glared up at the assassin as the serpents propelled him forward, head lopsided, mouth trickling blood down onto his body. He continued to be propelled by the four serpents and the tale that had emerged from his belly where his most terrible wound had been dealt. Hardrad was still deadly. His blood-speckled pale form was still immensely strong. The muscles were tense and giant as they aided the scaly fanged heads being projected from them. The tremendous human torso and head were still present amidst the reptilian projections, but they were not capable of locomotion without the scaly projections.

Michael used his flaming sword to sever the tail before it could coil around him. He then destroyed the two attacking serpents of the right stump, but a third emerged to confront him. When he had finally destroyed all the serpents on the right, he focused on this point of exposure. He slashed the head of the king and sliced at the body, and stabbed through the chest in search of Hardrad's black heart, but the effort only served to make him appear more grotesque. The other two serpents on the left were the strongest, but Michael destroyed one of them after a prolonged struggle. Only one head remained, and the king would finally die with its destruction.

The last serpent contained what remained of Hardrad's intelligence, and it desperately coiled itself around Michael's waist, lifting him high and digging fangs into him. Michael broke free with his own strength, and Hardrad knew the assassin could no longer be his prey. So, knowing evil could not prevail, the last serpent tried to drag the remains of the body away with a trail of blood, but Michael would not permit the Sephric to escape. He stood before the path of the king's body, his heart pounding with gratification at the final necessary deed, and swung down with his sword against the last serpent head. As the last drops of evil seeped out onto the stone in the black pool of blood beneath the dark sky, Michael knew he had finally vanquished the Sephric foe and driven out the blood of evil. He kicked the immense torso down, watched the pernicious flame die in Hardrad's pale eyes as they stared up at him, and finally made one last strike with his sword, severing the bearded skull from the blood-splattered mass of muscle left of Hardrad.

Michael looked down in triumph on the hacked grimace of the fallen king, its eyes screwed shut and forked tongue exposed, and waded through the dark pool of the monster's unrepentant evil blood in departure. The soldiers of Rose would find this mighty corpse, and know that the evil master of Hydra had already succumbed to the blade of the mysterious assassin. They would have much to celebrate upon discovery of this joyous sight, and know of the definite accomplishment of peace.

The battle continued to rage, and the Rose soldiers finally managed to break down the gates of the Hydran capital. They entered the city with heavy resistance, and battled through every corridor of the palace. Valdemar led his soldiers courageously through the palace.

Valdemar found the body of Hardrad on the top of the keep, and looked down on the blood-splattered pale rictus of his vanquished opponent. But he did not destroy the head or the body. Instead, he had the head placed on a pike and paraded around the celebrating soldiers of Rose, who jeered upon their sight of it and demanded it to be pulverised. Valdemar did not allow that act of the complete destruction of the relic to occur, however, for he derived satisfaction from the head's preservation. Valdemar died under mysterious circumstances soon after these events. It was never known what ultimately became of the Hardrad relic, but a whole wave of rumours permeated the Rose and Westcross societies over this matter.

The events for Michael were different. A voice came upon Michael, when he had vanquished Hardrad, and said, 'did you think I was really as weak as this, Guidonis?'

Michael did not know who was speaking, but he believed it was more powerful than even he, and so he became overwhelmed by a desire to escape this terrible stronghold soon. He did not want to find more horrific truths behind the nature of the Sephrics. Such a quest would be endless, and surely lead into the depths of the Undergrave itself. Even with all his sorcery-aided strengths and abilities, he believed he was no match for the titanic entity speaking. It was not visible, yet he was aware of its nefarious presence all around him. 'You had a thousand years to prepare a way to confront me again, and this tortured and misshapen entity is all you were able to come up with?'

Acknowledging this terrible being before them, the robed figure of Guidonis stepped out of the shadows and confided in Michael's ear, 'look above you. There is a spire at the very top of the High Tower. Your quest's end is before you. You must dispatch a sphere of flame against it, and be certain it is destroyed. Make fire as strong as you are able.'

Michael's eyes came upon the diabolical architecture of the spire and the turbulent sky whirling endlessly above, which began to send lightning into the structure as though somehow bestowing it with otherworldly powers. 'Destroy it now!' Guidonis commanded, and Michael focused his mind on his tense hand's sorcery as it manifested an orb of pure flame. He held his palm horizontally far, before his body, as he and his guide watched the bright sphere of destructive power materialise. At last, Michael looked in determination and rage at the spire. And he released the ball of flame against the pinnacle of the tower, just as it began to anchor a ghostly green discharge of energy from the violent clouds. The ensuing blast was catastrophic, but nowhere near as bizarre as the ensuing results, because this deed took the curtain of illusion away from the whole world, and all was revealed in its reality.

At it appeared to the warrior within the Dark Plane, the entire war and the entire political scenario had been a ruse. There was no Castle of the Sephrics at this location, nor had there ever been. In reality, only the fierce tempest above had been real. Here, at the supposed site of the stronghold, there stood nothing but a titanic crater housing some terrible multiple armed entity, the hideous progenitor of all the serpents Michael had slain, responsible for all the mischief that had ever come upon these lands. It is not certain how much of the quest was an illusion constructed by the creature's devices, but it appeared certain the Battle of Castle Sephric never occurred. The whole story of a Rose invasion was a ruse to give Michael and Guidonis a false sense of security. The Rose could never really have taken the Deathly Highway and marched to Hardrad's gates, even if their armies had proven strong enough to pierce the black heart of Hydra. For the latter half of his quest, Michael now realised, he had been wandering in illusions within illusions. Perhaps even Guidonis had been blind to this reality. The Sephric progenitor had cloaked itself behind a complex, elaborate illusion. There was no *House of Sephric.* In its ambition to rule over humanity, the real entity had constructed its image as a mighty noble

197

house residing at a castle, which sent out ruthless lords to govern mankind as slaves. In reality, there was a single main entity, the Progenitor, and all the Sephric lords Michael had slain were nothing more than the lesser serpent creatures the real entity had spawned to do its bidding.

'What is this monster?' Michael said, approaching the shapeless being in the pit. It anchored the continuing stream of green energy coming from the turbulent sky, by means of an array of black hooks, the probable teeth of the entity, surrounding the abyss of the central aperture.

'I am the Sephric,' the monster responded, 'young fool, all you have seen is very entertaining, but it was nothing but an illusion. You are nothing. You cannot slay me. Guidonis has brought you here to kill me, but he is a worse threat to this dream world of yours than I. You are his puppet foremost. Other than that, you are a corpse. You died back there when your home was destroyed, and you have nothing but vengeful impulses to guide you. That body is supposed to be in the Undergrave! You must take it there or Guidonis will take it from you, and your soul will go to the Undergrave instead. It is the will of the Constructor.'

'You have brought evil into the world. You are not from the Constructor,' Michael said, 'I am sworn and appointed by sorcery to fight you,' and he readied his hands with fire as he heard the call of the bat coming to aid him. He released the flames against the creature, but it was not harmed. Knowing it could not deter the assassin, the Sephric reached out with its spiny projections to slay the human. Michael was not touched, for he had not attacked unwisely. His bat mount arrived and swept him up from the ground. Devoid of bodily limitations, Guidonis glided close to the body, as the flaming sword was driven to sever the arms of the otherworldly being responsible for sending out so much evil across the land.

The proclamation of the creature about its own invulnerability was not true, for it was being destroyed by the green energy it had appeared to be harnessing. The destruction of spire had been the only thing necessary for the creature's destruction, for that instrument had evidently served to regulate the green energy safely. The green energy had been necessary for it to remain animate, and the energy had been regulated. To defend itself against Michael and Guidonis, it had no choice but to keep using the green energy to remain animate. Because the green energy entered it unregulated, the creature was severely harmed by its effects, and became motionless in death. Upon its destruction, the creature sank into what appeared to be a central aperture in the crater of its occupation, and this aperture closed with its disappearance into the earth. It was claimed by the soil, and the sky over the lands of Hydra became increasingly dark and violent after the cessation of the green fire from its midst.

Michael's body wandered the earth restlessly for some days after the Sephric Progenitor entity's demise, uncertain of his purpose. The absolute destruction of the Progenitor was never verifiable as a certainty, but Michael began to loathe his continued existence after the completion of the quest. His existence had been justified only by in the incompleteness of the quest, and so its completion brought him utter purposelessness.

Finally, they left the hazy Dark Plane and returned to the temporal plane, where they witnessed the ruins of the Castle of Hardrad. 'You must abandon the body now, Michael,' Guidonis spoke in a strong voice as the storm began to create roaring torrents of rain and howling winds that quenched the fires of the fallen castle in the temporal plane, and bade the hosts of Rose to end their celebrations and return to the pacification of the realm of the enemy.

'What is the hour?' Michael whispered on the sixth day after the death of Hardrad, looking at the sky, because it was filled with dark clouds circling fast above, and a poisonous fume seemed to also be mixing with the rain, turning it black and foul, and he did not know why. He wondered if the night was coming fast, as he beheld the terrible darkness that had come. After disposing of the bodies of the slaughtered horde of Hydra, the Rose host had departed quickly, taking all their artillery, in fear of the wrath the sky might pour on them for sacking the castle of the terrible Sephrics. Certainly, they were reacting to the black rain with horror, in the belief that it was a new evil upon them. And a new evil it was, for there was now only one accursed object left to destroy. A body standing dark and hooded beneath the storm. The cursed body of Michael. 'Now it is the hour that I will go to my right fate,' Michael accepted, piously. 'The Undergrave can be the only resting place of this evil instrument we call the body. It must be taken to the fires in the mountains, from whence the serpent founders of Hydra originated, who necessitated this quest, and cast back into the heart of evil. It will be destroyed utterly, for the good of all. My fate is terrible, but it is the price I pay for my part in the heretical methods that we have employed!'

Guidonis objected, not wanting the body gone, because the quest had hitherto served his own deadly ambitions, and thus did he want it to continue. He wished to continue poisonously deceiving his vassal into keeping the body here, because he had been seeking to use it to conquer his own wicked base of power. He said, 'do not be a fool! You know nothing of the Undergrave! There is another way. I seek the body, for the good of us both. We must work together and cohabit it. We are equals, as we have been throughout this quest, and we have a duty to protect the world from the intrusions of the creatures that do not belong here. So long as we are gone from the world, all good things are at risk to evil powers intruding into the world. And if you cast the body into the Undergrave, evil will find it, and use it to return to the world! All that you fought for will be lost again!'

But the heretic's designs had ever been as evil as his practices, and the light of truth forming in Michael's mind permitted his sister's honest voice to come quietly through the monk's curtain of deception. 'He lies!'

Michael looked fearfully at the sinister monk, in disillusionment, and said, 'you can kill the body, because I will no longer serve you, heretic! I hereby release you from this accursed carcass, and I pray that it dies fast without your sorcery maintaining it!'

'I do not intend to let the body die!' Guidonis yelled at him, dispatching a sphere of fire, but Michael raised his hands and froze the air, so that the approaching flames were quenched. 'You cannot defend your place in the body against me,' Guidonis said, 'if you don't surrender, I will oust you from it! I am the reason you are still in one piece! I am the wiser one, and the body is mine. Give it to me!'

'I will see it in the darkest pit of hell, first, even if we must both incur the consequence of concealment from all light and creation, in eternal torment. I will risk no portion of this flesh surviving in the world, lest you make an instrument of it for your evil ways.'

'Do not speak such nonsense! You know nothing of the despair that you will find if you carry out this ridiculous act!'

'I know all things, now, and you should be silent! You take me for a fool, and you intend to distort my understanding of reality and lead me astray. I will have no room for any thought other than burying you in the deepest pit of suffering and eternal death. Before, you cast my sister out of the quest, because your power over the body was growing, and she was trying to warn me. She was only your first target. Now, you wish to cast me out so that you possess the body entirely. You have ever been the real malice behind the ills of the world! You are the demon who manipulated me, and caused every evil that I have endured. I see your designs! I see what you did, in the beginning! You are an ancient being. That is why you possess such great power. Two centuries ago, when war was never necessary, you led the Hydrans to our lands, specifically to manufacture the crisis that would eventually permit you to perform your disgusting experiment on human flesh, and you chose me as your victim. I was a young man, mortally wounded, clinging to life, plagued by demons, with an unrelenting desire for vengeance, but my own mortality dictated that I would never achieve it. You only exploited my blind hatred, so that you could achieve your own goals. But you have underestimated your former vassal! I will fight you, and bring every pain to you that you brought upon others! Let the breaking of your malefic curses release my sister from her prison of ice, so she can be at peace. The Harvester will return to claim us, but I will have disposed of our wretched souls long before it gets to us! I may be damned already, but I can still release you, Berenice! Forgive me, and go over to the fairer realm waiting for you, where you will be away, out of sight from the outer darkness that is going to be the place of rest for these two heretics!'

XI. FINAL HARVEST

And so the withering body of Michael and the enduring spirit of Guidonis used their sorcery to exchange fire and ice, and darkness and light, and their duel took them all the way back onto the walls and turrets of the castle of the wicked Sephrics. At the highest place, on the cracked stone top of the Hydran castle's keep, Michael called out to the bat that had been his mount before, and, after some hours of battle with Guidonis through the rainy night, it came to him from the dark clouds, at last, sweeping him up and taking him high into the violent storm. But, as he ascended, he felt the following spirit of Guidonis, and knew that this demon was inescapable. The heretic was chained to the body, and was nearly in possession of it. But that possession would never be complete, because Michael would find the fiery pit where the serpent progenitors of evil had originated in the Mountain of the North, and he would cast the body there, to satiate the hunger of the very devils that birthed the heretical sorcery binding it. During their turbulent passage through the black storm, the flying spirit of the insidious monk followed him on the wind, and he approached his fiery grave at the Hydran volcano.

Although he could not see the flaming mountain, as he approached, he knew that he would find it, because it was the hungry cauldron of the storm, and the storm's centre was the only exit from his evil state of existence. The Undergrave craved for his coming, and he was driven to answer its call. So he never saw the volcano, and nor did he catch sight of any ashes or brimstone, but he had a sudden glimpse of shadow and flame, and he collided with his target. The faithful bat was the mount of a sorcerer, built to journey to the darkest parts of the universe, so it did not deny him the right to take it to the other side with him. The passage through was instantaneous, and it did not merely burn them up in the searing heat of a volcano like one would expect from the ruinous act, because this was no ordinary volcanic vent capable of dealing death to one who falls in, but a real door to the second death for anyone who takes it.

When they exited, on the other side, their place was in a circle of fire, and writhing masses of dark serpents surrounded them, beyond it, in the shadows. But the duelling heretics cared not for their location, because they were committed only to destroy one another. Michael told him, 'you will never inhabit this body now, Guidonis. It might not be able to die the first death in the world outside, but I have taken it to the world beneath. I have circumvented its regeneration, by taking it into the darkness that nothing can escape from. I will lose it in the darkest shadows of the universe and you will never find it!'

'You have succeeded only in taking us to your own soul's final resting place, Michael,' the heretic replied, 'I have ways of escaping the Undergrave, for I have resided here before. You will take my place in torment, and the body will leave with me. Surrender it!'

'Only if you can endure the pain!' Michael resisted, dashing through the barrier of flame, so that he went among the black serpents, but they retreated from him in terror, and made a path for him towards a great stone stairway, lit by burning beacons that led to the top of a crumbling city, beneath the tortured crimson sky. The Undergrave Nexus was calling to him. There, he would seek counsel from the guarantors of eternal death, so that he could attain it and escape the evil designs of Guidonis. He would seal his fate, and the fate of his enemy, by locking the evil entity known as Guidonis in the most terrible place of shadow and flame, that same place that had surely birthed and maintained the sorcerer's evil ways.

They came to the iron gates of the Undergrave Nexus, which were adorned with the frightening depictions of the dead who dwelt here, and they opened in answer to the body's presence, allowing him passage into the citadel. He passed, with his sword still flaming in his hand, and Guidonis pursued him and hurled spheres of fire with equal destructive power. Again, they exchanged the bewitched fire of their hands, but neither of them could assail the other, for they were fighting in a place of already assured annihilation. Neither could perish, while they existed only as tormented beings in the Undergrave Nexus. The citadel was unoccupied, because its creatures had all fled from the fearsome duelling sorcerers, so Michael continued to the bridge beyond.

Guarding with his fiery sword against Guidonis as he stepped backwards, he looked down from the bridge, and saw a river of fire, with columns of poisonous fume rising, and the writhing forms of men and unrecognisable creatures in its depths. Among these demonic forms, there were winged pretas. Knowing these were the creatures that had first plagued him, and they had made the ritual of Guidonis necessary to purge them and heal the body, he believed that they might be capable of undoing the body. They might not be capable of assailing the body, but it would complicate the plans of Guidonis, if he plunged into the fires of the red river below. He did not fear his fate.

He allowed himself to fall, but he was shocked to find that he did not fall into the river's fire. He felt the claws and teeth of hungry entities harass and tear at the body, but the flesh merely healed again and was denied the conclusion that would have been possible if he and Guidonis had simply vaporised in the searing heat. The most torturous thing was to know that Guidonis was constantly locked in his pursuit. Instead of a final end in the fires of the red stream, a dark mouth opened in it, and they were both enveloped in shadow. The river did not claim them. Instead, they fell into a chasm of dark stone, which was cold. They landed in a hollow of complete darkness. It was mostly silent as they wrestled, except for the occasional echo of the sniffles of sorrowful souls condemned to dwell in their sorrow there.

The darkness in the hollow was interrupted by a bright incursion of red fire and wings from an aperture in the stone, and pretas descended on the two heretics, hurling fire onto them, but they were not affected. Demons came in a great swarm to fiercely overwhelm the sorcerers, but the agents of death were unsuccessful. Michael led the fray to a guardian creature, which took the form of a towering being much mightier than Hardrad. It possessed so many serpentine heads that Michael could not count them, but no sooner could he begin than they immediately coiled around the bodies of both he and Guidonis, and lifted them. Although he wanted the body destroyed,

Michael wanted to see of Guidonis first, so he did not permit the creature to subject him to its regimen of eternal Undergrave Nexus torture.

There was little conclusiveness to the duel of Michael and Guidonis, who continued to wage their war throughout the eternally vast Undergrave, which took them through cold chambers of despair and hot dungeons of torture. They fought ferociously in lakes of boiling blood, through titanic dungeons, and over expanses of flaming molten rock. There was no end to their quest to annihilate one another. The body was lost from the rock of the world that it had known, but it would never rest. The conflict of the heretic-sorcerers, each at the other's throat, would be unending. They would go on, in their mutual annihilation, just like the shadows, the fires, and the sounds of grief that had engulfed them.

It is believed that Michael and Guidonis earned a permanent place in the Undergrave. Forever, they continued their duel across the vast eternal battlefields of all the hells, pursued by demons and devoured by the guardians and harvesters as they went on. Such was the ultimate fate accorded to them by the guarantors of eternal destruction, in whose technologies they had placed so much faith.

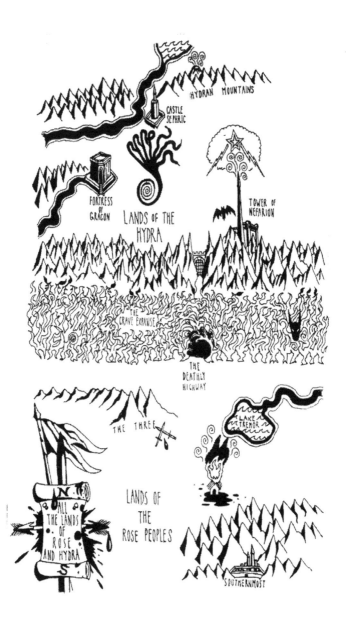

Made in the USA
Lexington, KY
14 September 2011